T N TRAYNOR

The Mistletoe Heist

A Winterbourne Hall Mystery

This is a work of fiction.

Names, characters, businesses, places, events and incidents either are the products of the author's imagination or used in a fictitious manner.

Any resemblance to actual persons, living or dead, or actual events is purely coincidental.

T. N. Traynor
Publishing

First Printed Edition, England February 2025
ISBN: 9798313626512

2

Book Description

A Christmas house party, a stolen heirloom, and a deadly game. But when everyone is hiding something, who can one trust?

Eleanor Carstone never imagined herself as a thief, but when she attends a Regency-themed murder mystery weekend at Winterbourne Hall, she finds herself entangled in a real-life heist. The priceless Mistletoe Bauble, a cherished family heirloom, has disappeared without a trace. With suspicion falling on Eleanor, she must race against time to uncover the truth before being wrongfully accused of the crime.

Surrounded by a winter wonderland and a group of guests with their own secrets, Eleanor teams up with investigative journalist Nathaniel Blackwood to solve the mystery. Their partnership is uneasy—Nathaniel is sharp, guarded, and far too perceptive for Eleanor's liking—but as they navigate a web of deception, a hidden passageway, and a tricky murder mystery game that may be a stepping stone to finding the thief, an undeniable spark forms between them.

Yet, with the snow falling and tensions rising, trust is a dangerous thing. As the line between game and reality blurs, will Eleanor and Nathaniel solve the case before it's too late? And will their growing feelings survive the truth when it finally comes to light?

For fans of cosy mysteries, atmospheric country house settings, and sweet, slow-burn romances, *The Mistletoe Heist* is a thrilling read that will keep you on the edge of your seat until the very end. Don't miss out on this suspenseful holiday tale—buy now before the price changes!

If you enjoy books like *And Then There Were None* by Agatha Christie and *Pride and Prejudice* by Jane Austen, you'll love this Christmas romance *The Mistletoe Heist* by T N Traynor.

Index

MRS WINTERBOURNE

invites you to

WINTERBOURNE HALL

MURDER MYSTERY WEEKEND

FRIDAY 12 TO SUNDAY 14 DECEMBER

FOR A MOST DIVERTING WEEKEND OF REGENCY
AMUSEMENT FROM FOUR O'CLOCK IN THE
AFTERNOON ON FRIDAY UNTIL LATE SUNDAY
AFTERNOON GUESTS ARE MOST PARTICULARLY
REMINDED THAT FOR FRIDAY AND SATURDAY
DINNER, AS WELL AS SUNDAY LUNCHEON, ATTIRE IN
THE REGENCY FASHION IS A STRICT REQUIREMENT.

MRS. WINTERBOURNE IS DELIGHTED TO
EXTEND THE HOSPITALITY OF HER
HUMBLE ABODE AND LOOKS FORWARD
TO THE PLEASURE OF YOUR
ACQUAINTANCE.

Chapter 1

MISS ELEANOR CARSTONE had not intended to become a thief. And yet, here she stood in the grand ballroom of Winterbourne Hall, listening to a choir singing carols, her gaze fixed on the very object she might be required to steal. She could not help but marvel at how circumstances had conspired to place her in such a predicament.

The bauble resided in a purpose-built, locked glass cabinet—a solitary display that only heightened its significance. Invitees gathered nearby, their expressions a mix of admiration and something dangerously close to greed. Eleanor doubted she was the only one entranced by it.

The display cabinet sat amongst other historical curiosities, but the delicate, tennis-ball-sized ornament was a masterpiece of craftsmanship. Silver mistletoe leaves adorned the glass sphere, and within, a golden key lay entwined with white gold and pearl mistletoe. The intricate design formed an ethereal glow as it caught the light.

She took a sip of her mulled wine. If one was going to contemplate larceny, one might as well be comfortably warm whilst doing so.

"Miss Carstone, I trust everything is alright?"

Turning, she discovered Mr Blake Cunningham, the recently appointed estate caretaker, watching her with an amused, polite expression. In his deep green waistcoat and expertly knotted cravat, his impeccable Regency attire suggested a character lifted from the pages of Jane Austen. Unfortunately, his sharp eyes suggested he missed next to nothing.

Eleanor's lips curved into a smile; the kind of smile th. once convinced an elderly museum curator to grant her access to a restricted archive. The candelabra's light caught the silken sheen of her gown, the deep sapphire fabric draped with an elegant flair over her figure. The gown's empire waistline and delicately scalloped neckline, trimmed with the finest lace, lent her an air of timeless grace.

"Mr Cunningham. You must forgive me—I was quite lost in appreciation." She lifted a lace gloved hand and pointed at the display.

"Ah, yes. The Mistletoe Bauble. It has a rather romantic history and more than one rumour attached to it."

Pretending she had not spent weeks researching it, Eleanor asked, "Does it?"

He leaned in, lowering his voice. "Legend has it, if two people share a kiss beneath it, they will be bound together for life."

Eleanor snorted. "How terribly inconvenient."

"Indeed." His gaze flickered, almost imperceptibly, towards the cabinet's lock. Then, as though remembering himself, he straightened. "But I suspect you are more interested in its craftsmanship than its folklore."

She met his eyes and smiled again. "Naturally."

At that precise moment, a bloodcurdling scream rang out from the upper gallery.

A collective gasp rippled through the ballroom, and Eleanor turned swiftly, setting her crystal goblet aside. Somewhere in the house, a woman shrieked for help. A flurry of movement followed, with participants lifting their skirts or unbuttoning their tailcoats in preparation of some heroic (or nosey) sprinting.

Blake Cunningham wasted no time as he strode out of the ballroom into the massive hallway that held the grand staircase, Eleanor close on his heels. He glanced back only once, catching her with a look that was both wary and intrigued.

"I do hope, Miss Carstone, that you were not contemplating any mischief this evening."

Eleanor, who had been, widened her eyes with the picture of innocence. "Mr Cunningham, how could you think such a thing?" That her mind raced with devising a plan to get the infamous bauble into her hands, she kept to herself.

Half-expecting murder, mayhem, or a ghost, Eleanor quickened her pace toward the screams, her heartbeat quickening despite knowing the situation would not be real. Coming to a halt, she found herself staring at the cause of the ruckus. A young woman in an emerald-green gown fluttered her fan with much gusto in front of her heaving bosom. The striking blonde, with perfectly sculptured curls, clutched her throat and staggered back against the mahogany balustrade.

A gentleman in a black waistcoat and breeches came alongside Eleanor, his expression torn between diversion and disinterest. "Oh, for heaven's sake," he chuntered at her elbow.

Glancing over her shoulder, she saw a man in his mid-thirties, impeccably dressed in the style of Mr Darcy, right down to the cravat that looked too complicated for anyone to have tied without help. Unlike the others, he appeared distinctly unimpressed. His dark brows lifted as he took in Eleanor's wide-eyed expression.

"I assume she's part of the entertainment and the *fun* has begun," he said dryly, nodding at the blonde woman, who now swooned artfully into the arms of her companion. "Unless, of course, someone genuinely expired over the apéritifs."

Eleanor's pulse settled. "It's a murder mystery weekend. If someone doesn't start screaming at some point, I suppose we would all feel short-changed."

A faint smirk touched his lips. "Indeed. Although, I wonder if Mrs Winterbourne instructed her actors to be quite so..." He grinned as the blonde let out a second, rather theatrical gasp. "Melodramatic."

At the mention of their hostess, Eleanor scanned the room. Mrs Winterbourne, ever the grand lady of the house, appeared at the top of the staircase. Pausing just long enough to ensure all eyes turned her way, she descended with a graceful flourish, the rich burgundy fabric of her gown rustling as she moved. Petite and in her late sixties, she carried herself like a queen surveying her kingdom—one that had, regrettably, fallen into disrepair but remained magnificent, nonetheless.

"My dear friends!" she announced, her voice rich and musical. "Fear not! This is simply my way of gaining your attention. There will be numerous dark and dastardly events this weekend, but as dear Mama always said... refreshments first, chaos second!" She clapped her gloved hands together. "A murder most foul will take place somewhere in Winterbourne Hall this evening. It is your task to uncover the villain responsible! But first... mulled wine and mince pies!"

A ripple of excitement went through the assembled guests, and as the tension eased, Eleanor found herself smiling.

The man beside her chuckled softly. "Her devotion to the role is nothing short of remarkable."

"It is," Eleanor agreed. "Though to be fair, I have heard she wears Regency clothes whether there is an event on or not."

He studied their hostess with an appraising look. "You know, I heard that too, but dismissed it as too far-fetched. But seeing her now... well, I can rather believe it."

9

Before Eleanor could reply, a butler—an actual butler—stepped forward with a silver tray of drinks. Mr Donald Grady, tall and impeccably composed, moved with a precision that suggested he had anticipated the need before it arose, his pale blue gaze coolly assessing the room without seeming to look at anyone directly.

The man beside her reached for two glasses and offered one to her.

"Since we seem to be kindred spirits in observing the absurdity of it all," he said, his words flowing with effortless charm, "I suppose I should introduce myself. Nathaniel Blackwood."

Eleanor accepted the glass as she measured the man before her. "Eleanor Carstone."

He inclined his head in practised Regency elegance. "A pleasure, Miss Carstone."

Unbidden, a warm sensation blossomed in her chest. Winterbourne Hall, with its flickering candlelight, pine and spice scents, and crumbling grandeur, created an atmospheric setting, especially with its impressive Victorian-style Christmas decorations. And Nathaniel Blackwood, with his sharp wit and unreadable expression, might just be the most intriguing character in the room.

*****

The assembled attendees acknowledged their approval as servers distributed more wine, and the rich scent of cinnamon and cloves filled the air as they gathered in the hall. Eleanor refused a third glass with a polite shake of her head, and accepted a glass of cordial instead, her thoughts occupied with the treasure encased in its glass prison.

Winterbourne Hall was a place of contradictions. Its sumptuousness, dulled by years of neglect, stood in contrast to the two years of Mrs Winterbourne's ongoing restorations. Polished furniture stood alongside timeworn pieces, new carpets replaced threadbare ones only in the rooms now open to the public. The chandeliers, once dazzling, shimmered only half-heartedly, their crystals clouded with dust. Only a portion of Winterbourne Hall was ready for visitors, while the rest of the estate needed various repairs—a challenge Mrs Winterbourne was determined to overcome—thus the fundraising events.

Nathaniel Blackwood lingered at Eleanor's side, sipping his wine with the air of one amused by the spectacle yet apart from it. "Tell me, Miss Carstone," he mused, his voice carrying the faintest note of mischief, "are you in the habit of attending such theatrics? Or is it purely the enticement of Winterbourne Hall that drew you here?"

Eleanor turned to him with an arch smile. "Oh, I am but an innocent observer, Mr Blackwood. Though, if I were to confess, I would say I am rather a fan of mysteries. But most of all, I am a student of human nature, if you will."

His dark eyes flickered with interest. "Ah. An admirable pastime."

Despite his presence at the Hall's murder mystery event, Eleanor knew he mocked her beneath his composed exterior. Though a trifle irked, she decided not to take the bait and smiled in what she hoped was a charming manner.

She inclined her head demurely. "And yourself? What do you do for a living? Do you make it a habit to attend events of this nature, or are you here for some other purpose?"

"A most excellent question." He swirled his wine thoughtfully. "Let us say that I, too, am a student of human nature. And, perhaps, of Mrs Winterbourne's eccentricities. It is not often one finds a hostess who so willingly transforms her home into a stage of Jane Austen ilk and flavour."

Eleanor was about to reveal her online research, which uncovered a hobby previously unknown to her—Janeites, Jane Austen fans who attend Regency events, when she caught sight of the estate manager bee lining straight for her.

Blake Cunningham moved through the gathering with the quiet efficiency of a man accustomed to managing chaos. When he reached her, his gaze settled on her with polite curiosity. "Miss Carstone, I trust you have found the evening entertaining thus far?"

"Indeed, Mr Cunningham, a most lively affair." Although her attention stayed on the steward, she was acutely aware of Mr Blackwood's proximity and the way he watched her.

Blake nodded, then addressed the guests more broadly. "For those of you that are new to Winterbourne Hall, I am happy to answer any questions regarding its history. Though only a portion of the house is open, much of its past remains intact." He gestured toward the far wall, where several portraits of Winterbourne ancestors presided over the evening's revelries with solemn disapproval. "Many of these gentlemen—and ladies—once walked these halls, no doubt hosting events of a more dignified nature."

Nathaniel smirked. "A shame none of them left behind a ledger detailing their misdeeds. It would make for excellent reading."

Blake's lips twitched. "Indeed, Mr Blackwood. Though perhaps *some* secrets are best left to the imagination."

Eleanor, her thoughts still fixed upon the bauble, seized the opportunity. "And the collection of curiosities? Are they all part of the family's legacy?"

Blake hesitated for the briefest of moments before replying. "Most of them, yes. Others have been acquired over the years through donations or acquisitions. The Mistletoe Bauble that caught your eye, for instance, was gifted to Mrs Winterbourne some twenty years ago."

"How fortunate," Eleanor said, her fingers tapping on the stem of her glass.

"Indeed." With a slight bow, he moved on.

Nathaniel observed her with idle curiosity. "You seem particularly interested in it, Miss Carstone."

She met his gaze with perfect equanimity. "It is a rather remarkable piece."

Before he could reply, Mr Grady rang a small bell at the doorway into the drawing room and cleared his throat with theatrical solemnity. "Ladies and gentlemen, Mrs Winterbourne requests your presence for the commencement of the evening's entertainment," announced the butler in full pomp.

The guests stirred, murmuring in anticipation as they began to move to the appointed room. Eleanor followed, her mind still working through the puzzle before her. Undoubtedly, the bauble was the piece that she had come to verify. Retrieving it, if indeed it proved to be stolen, would require both cunning and care. Once in her possession, she would hand the item over to the police for them to investigate its true ownership.

And yet, something about this gathering—the staged theatrics, the curated eccentricities of their hostess—made her doubt that Mrs Winterbourne knew she owned a stolen artefact. For who puts stolen goods on display? It would be good if she could stay at the house for more than two nights to do some digging around.

As she stepped into the drawing-room, Nathaniel once again at her side, she had the distinct sensation that she was not the only one with secrets to keep.

＊＊＊＊＊

As Mr Grady collected empty glasses and supplied a fresh round of drinks, Eleanor took the opportunity to reflect on her fellow attendees. It was apparent they fell into one of two categories—those who had flung themselves into the spirit of the occasion with the fervour of devoted disciples, and those who had been dragged along in various states of resignation.

The Janeites—true devotees of their hostess's beloved literary world—had spared no effort in their appearance. The women wore high-waisted gowns in silks and muslins. Some elegant and subdued, others in shades so bright that even Mrs Winterbourne's own flamboyant taste would be hard-pressed to rival. Hair had been painstakingly arranged in curls and braids, often adorned with ribbons or pearl combs. More than one lady carried a delicate fan, which they fluttered with the air of nobility who had practised extensively before a looking glass.

The gentlemen were a more curious study. Some had embraced the masquerade with as much enthusiasm as their wives. Their coats and waistcoats rich with embroidery, and their boots polished to an enviable gleam.

A few had even attempted the difficult art of the cravat, though with varying degrees of success. Others, however, carried the unmistakable air of men who had suffered an onslaught of coaxing, cajoling, or outright coercion in order to be pressed into their Regency finery. Their breeches were stiff, their tailcoats sat awkwardly upon their shoulders, and their cravats had clearly been tied by hands other than their own— most likely under duress.

Eleanor took a slow sip of her cordial, pondering which of these men had been the most reluctant to surrender their modern comforts. She imagined several had protested with varying excuses: the difficulty of fastening breeches, the indignity of heeled boots, or the sheer absurdity of parading about in a coat that required so many buttons. And yet here they all were, some bearing it with good humour, others with the weary resignation of a man who had long since learned that resistance was futile.

The strains of a string quartet accompanied her musings. At the far end of the drawing room, four musicians played a lively rendition of Mozart's *Eine kleine Nachtmusik*. The bright, cheerful notes danced through the air, filling the space with an energy that was both refined and invigorating.

The violins led with crisp precision, the viola and cello weaving harmonies that lent a rich depth to the melody. It was a tune both familiar and agreeable, one that set toes tapping and heads nodding in time. A few of the ladies swayed, their skirts whispering against the floor like reeds bending in a soft breeze, as though they longed to be whisked onto the dance floor.

Into this harmonious scene, Lady Genevieve's voice rose, clear and commanding, ensuring all within earshot turned their attention to her. "Did you hear? A man was hanged at Aylesbury in Buckinghamshire for highway robbery, but last week. A dreadful affair." She gave a theatrical sigh, the feathers of her fan fluttering as she pressed it to her bosom.

"A just end for such a villain," remarked a gentleman standing nearby. "These wretches terrorise the roads, preying upon the innocent."

Lady Genevieve cast him a look of mild reproach and snapped her fan shut. "Indeed, but not all are so lacking in refinement. I myself was robbed but six months ago. To my relief, he was a Gentleman's Master and not a Bully Ruffian— his manners were quite impeccable, I assure you! Had the

15

circumstances been otherwise, I might have considered it a most thrilling adventure."

"Unscrupulous muggers, all of them." Mrs Dunlop sniffed and flapped her fan with much verve. "No better than common cutpurses lurking in alleyways." She stopped flapping to dab her gleaming cheeks with her handkerchief.

"Beastly lot," her husband interjected, waving a gloved hand with some agitation. A man in his late sixties, with silvered sideburns and a slight stoop that did little to curb his energy, he huffed. "No finesse in them at all! A true tradesman knows the worth of his wares. But daylight robbery by a scallion on horseback? Uncouth, quite vulgar." He gave a dismissive shake of his head, his expression one of deepest offence, as though the notion of such base criminality was an affront to his sensibilities.

After accepting a flute of Champagne from a passing waiter, Lady Genevieve arched a brow, her gaze lingering upon him a fraction longer than was necessary. "A most interesting perspective, Mr Dunlop. And may I ask—do you speak from experience?"

A ripple of amusement flickered through the gathering, though whether at Lady Genevieve's playful provocation or Mr Dunlop's apparent dismay, none could say. He gave a short, barking laugh and adjusted his cuffs. "I speak only as a man of business, madam. If one is to steal, one ought at least to do so with some degree of elegance."

"And what say you, Lord Whitmore, on the matter of highwaymen?" Genevieve's gaze fixed upon a tall gentleman attired in the finest evening dress, a deep blue velvet coat and an elaborate white ruff lending him a resplendent air, who happened to be standing close to Eleanor.

Eleanor, and indeed the rest of the assembly, turned their attention to him, their interest piqued. She studied his striking features—dark eyes set beneath an aristocratic brow, a faint curve of drollness at the corner of his lips—and caught the warm, citrus-laced scent of his cologne as it lingered in the air.

He met Genevieve's smile with a slow, deliberate raise of his glass. "I should think, madam," he said, his voice smooth as the finest port, "that there is a distinction between a gentleman of fortune and a mere common footpad. One has a certain... artistry in his craft, while the other is no better than a brute with a cudgel."

The remark was met with murmurs of approval and a smattering of laughter.

"And which, my lord, do you admire most?" The light from the chandeliers caught the glint of playfulness in her eyes.

Lord Ambrose Whitmore took a measured sip of his wine, his gaze never wavering. "Why, Lady Genevieve, that depends *entirely* on the success of his endeavours."

For the briefest moment, an unreadable expression flitted across her features. Then, with a practised flutter of her fan, she laughed, and the conversation turned to lighter topics with much merriment and laughter.

The next hour passed in a pleasant haze of conviviality. People gathered in small clusters, sipping wine and exchanging lively remarks, their voices mingling with the strains of a violin and cello as the musicians played a selection of well-loved airs. Servants moved deftly between them, replenishing glasses and offering delicate canapés upon silver trays.

As the grandfather clock struck seven, Mrs Winterbourne, wanting to capture the full attention of everyone, clapped her hands together.

"My dear friends," she announced, "you will each be given a small notebook and pencil. These are for your observations throughout the weekend. Make notes of your thoughts, your suspicions, and any dreadful secrets that may come to light. By the end of our game, your notes will be collected and you must put forward your accusations. The most astute detective among you shall be rewarded with a prize most worthy—a week's stay with us as our most honoured guest."

An excited clapping and cheering followed. Eleanor straightened. An extra week after the weekend would give her all the time she needed to fulfil her task. Suddenly, solving the game took on new importance.

A ripple of joviality spread through the assembly as footmen hired for the evening moved through the crowd, handing each guest a slim leather-bound notebook. Eleanor accepted hers with mild curiosity. The cover was embossed with an elegant gold monogram: Winterbourne Hall, Christmastide Mystery.

"A fine touch." Nathaniel flipped open his own book. "It lends the affair a sense of gravitas, as though we are embarking upon a most serious inquiry rather than a parlour game."

Eleanor smiled. "Indeed. And yet I cannot help but wonder if our hostess hides a secondary motive. Encouraging us to write our observations will surely make for an excellent record of her guests' wit and imagination—something she might later enjoy at her leisure."

Nathaniel's lips twitched. "A clever scheme, if that is her aim." He tapped his pencil against the page, then, in an exaggerated flourish, wrote his first line. "Mr Nathaniel Blackwood, astute observer of the absurd, notes that his companions have been suitably plied with wine and mince pies, and are now primed for intrigue."

Eleanor laughed but made no move to begin her own notes just yet.

The butler, at Mrs Winterbourne's side, called out in a loud voice, "Rooms and passageways adorned with a bunch of laurel branches or cornered off by a purple silken rope are off limits and still under repair. Besides bedrooms, the rest of the Hall presents itself to you as an open book."

Keeping everyone's attention, Mrs Winterbourne sensed the perfect moment to heighten the drama and lifted her hands. "And now, my dear friends, you shall be escorted to the library!"

Eleanor pushed the pencil back into the spine's pen holder and slipped her hand through the book's purple wristband. An ingenious design that meant the ladies could carry the books with them at all times while still leaving their hands free.

A delighted hush fell over the gathering. The quartet, as if on cue, shifted their melody into something more solemn— Beethoven's *Moonlight Sonata*, its haunting strains curling through the air like mist over the moors. The change in music cast a spell upon the room, and even those who had been jesting only moments before straightened their shoulders, adopting expressions of eager anticipation.

Donald Grady reappeared at Mrs Winterbourne's side, and with a grand sweep of his arm, "If you would be so good as to follow me, ladies and gentlemen."

Eleanor glanced at Nathaniel. His dark eyes gleamed with mirth, but there was something else there, too—an alertness, a quiet calculation, as though he were taking stock of the moment with the keen eye of someone who was here for something more than entertainment.

Following the others as they made their way along the passage, Eleanor wondered what lay ahead. If she wanted more time to uncover the truth of the Mistletoe Bauble, she would have to do her best to solve this murder mystery game!

Chapter 2

THE PROCESSION MOVED as one through the corridors of Winterbourne Hall, their hushed voices mingling with the fading strains of Beethoven's *Moonlight Sonata*. At the head of the party, the butler led them with solemn dignity, his expression deadpan despite the theatricality of the moment. The air was thick with the mingled scents of beeswax, evergreens, and the faint lingering aroma of spiced wine, while the flickering sconces cast elongated shadows along the panelled walls.

The company emerged into the library, and at once all eyes turned to the Christmas tree. Taller than any Eleanor had ever seen indoors, it reached to the ceiling, its boughs heavy with Victorian-style decorations. Glistening strands of glass beads caught the flickering light that bounced from the tall windows off the strategically placed mirrors.

Gilded pinecones and delicate porcelain cherubs nestled amongst the dark green branches. Paper angels, intricately made, swayed in the soft breeze caused by the flow of bodies. Golden ribbons held small glass bells, from which a faint tinkling sound arose when disturbed. The whole display was crowned by a grand star of cut glass, which refracted the warm glow of the room's many candles into a soft, shimmering light.

"A most magnificent specimen. I daresay one might require a ladder of no insignificant height to affix an ornament from halfway up."

Nathaniel's voice, low with appreciation, rolled with a depth that sparked instant appreciation in Eleanor. Her gaze swept over the tree, but her mind not on its magnificence, nor the sudden longing for Nathaniel's next words. It was on the bauble in the glass cabinet in the ballroom. Her meandering thoughts, however, were swiftly drawn from their course by a sudden gasp.

"My word!" cried the plump Mrs Dunlop, batting the sides of her elaborate velvet gown with quite some gusto. "She is quite—dead!"

All eyes turned in the direction of her exclamation, and Eleanor beheld the scene of their supposed crime.

Near the fireplace, sprawled upon the richly patterned Aubusson rug, lay the 'murder' victim. The actress was a striking woman with auburn curls, dressed in a deep green satin gown that pooled around her as if she had collapsed mid-reverie. One hand lay outstretched, fingers still clutching a silken handkerchief embroidered with the initial A. Beside her, a pool of crimson satin created the chilling illusion of a fatal wound.

"Lady Genevieve has been most foully dispatched," proclaimed Mrs Winterbourne, who had assumed the grave countenance of a coroner. "Struck upon the head with a blunt instrument, I am afraid."

A ripple of murmurs passed through the gathering.

"A blunt instrument, you say?" intoned Colonel Montague, an elderly gentleman whose military whiskers bristled with interest. "A fire-iron, perhaps?"

"Or a candlestick?" ventured Miss Leighton, her green eyes alight with glee.

Mrs Winterbourne smiled indulgently, lifting a gloved hand to command their attention. "You may each examine the scene before the police arrive, and I encourage you to take note of every detail. Do not disregard anything as insignificant—many a clue can be overlooked by those who fail to attend to the smallest of particulars." She turned as if to leave the room, but spun around with a flourish, causing her skirts to swish around her. With a delicate touch, she brushed back an unruly curl that had sprung from the otherwise perfect hair doo. "Oh, I forgot to mention, do get to know each other as well as you can... for one of you is a murderer!"

Eleanor needed no further encouragement. As the others stepped forward in small clusters, she drew closer to the 'corpse' and regarded the unfortunate Lady Genevieve with care. The positioning of the body, the silken handkerchief, the rich folds of green satin—all had been meticulously arranged, yet it was the expression on the actress's face that struck Eleanor the most. Though her eyes remained closed, there was a hint of a smirk at the corners of her lips, as though she were inwardly amused by her own demise.

"A rather contented victim, is she not?" Nathaniel said at her shoulder.

Eleanor stifled a laugh. "Perhaps she is wholly pleased to be lying down after the exertion of standing in that dress all evening."

He inclined his head, pointing out the actress's abandoned flute upon a side table, still half full of Champagne. "Then again, perhaps the murderer was not so brutish as to wield a weapon at all. A draught of poison might prove just as effective."

She raised an eyebrow. "But would that account for the blood?"

"Ah," he conceded with a grin. "A fair point."

A footman appeared and presented a silver tray to the assembled. Upon it lay several small envelopes, each marked with the name of a guest in elegant script.

"These," he announced, "contain your first clue. Mrs Winterbourne suggests you use them wisely."

Eleanor accepted hers with a small nod of thanks and withdrew to the far end of the room, where she broke the wax seal and unfolded the slip of paper within.

Though she danced as a leaf upon the floor...

It was not music that caused her fall.

Find the weapon, you'll have your next clue.

Remember—all clues to remain in situ.

Cryptic to be sure, but Eleanor had long been accustomed to unravelling tangled words and hidden meanings. The mention of dancing called to mind the grand ballroom, where they had gathered for the opening of the evening's festivities. Had the 'victim' last been seen there before her untimely demise?

She glanced up to find Nathaniel studying his own clue with a contemplative expression. At length, he approached her with an arch of his brow.

"Miss Eleanor," he said, lowering his voice so only she could hear, "it occurs to me that while the sport of detection may be engaging in solitude, two heads are most assuredly better than one."

She feigned mild disinterest. "Are you proposing an alliance, Mr Blackwood?"

"I suggest that we share our insights, lest some lesser intellect claim the prize before us."

Eleanor considered him for a moment. He was quick-witted, that much was certain, and she had little doubt that he possessed an aptitude for uncovering secrets. Yet she also had an inkling that his motivations, like her own, extended beyond the simple pleasure of the game.

She allowed a small smile. "As you wish, Mr Blackwood. We shall collaborate—for now."

He inclined his head. "A most excellent decision, Miss Carstone. Shall we…" he extended his own clue to her. She hesitated a moment before handing hers to him.

She glanced over at his clue.

> *The murderer may be many things,*
> *But a liar they are not. Be a wise inquisitor.*
> *NB. You may hand this card over and ask 'Are you*
> *the murderer' only once.*

"Do you think everyone will have a different clue?"

Nathaniel rubbed his chin. "Probably not. I should imagine there are a few different ones, though, to encourage us to mingle."

Eleanor scrunched up her face and Nathaniel burst out laughing.

"My thoughts exactly! Now, let us see if we cannot make short work of this mystery before supper, and before any of these well-dressed detectives should happen upon the solution before us."

*****

The dining room at Winterbourne Hall was a vision of warmth and festivity. A grand fire blazed in the great stone hearth, its golden light casting a flickering glow upon the high ceiling, where intricate plasterwork depicted garlands of holly and ivy entwined in an eternal embrace.

Above the mantel, a magnificent wreath of glossy holly leaves and rich red berries took pride of place, its deep green hues vibrant against the carved oak panelling. The scent of burning logs mingled with the enticing aroma of spiced meats and freshly baked bread, creating an atmosphere that was both elegant and inviting.

The table itself was a masterpiece of festive indulgence. A fine damask cloth of deep burgundy draped its length, its surface adorned with elegant, Roman-inspired candelabras whose wax tapers burned steadily, casting long shadows. At each setting, a tiny Christmas present, wrapped in paper embossed with golden stars, had been placed as a token of seasonal goodwill. The sight of them prompted delighted murmurs, and more than one guest turned theirs over in their hands with childlike curiosity.

Eleanor took her seat, her gaze sweeping over the assembled company. Despite the artifice of the evening's entertainment, there was an air of genuine excitement amongst everyone. Their faces alight with anticipation as the first course was served.

The meal was a wonderful, curated blend of tradition with a dash of modern indulgence. Platters of roast beef, glazed ham, and game pies carried forth by uniformed footmen, accompanied by bowls of buttered parsnips, creamed carrots, and spiced red cabbage. A tureen of steaming vegetable soup sat on a side table, and footmen offered baskets of bread rolls to everyone.

Yet amongst these traditional delights, Eleanor noted a few concessions to modern taste—tiny vol-au-vents, filled with delicate mushroom ragout, and an artfully arranged platter of smoked salmon, garnished with curls of lemon peel and the oddest addition of angel hair smothered in a Thai sauce.

"You appear most contemplative, Miss Carstone," Nathaniel's voice interrupted her thoughts. He had taken the seat beside her, his expression one of interest as he studied her over the rim of his wine glass.

She turned to him with a slight smile. "I am considering the effort expended in crafting such a meal. It is quite the spectacle."

"As indeed are most things at Winterbourne Hall, Mrs Winterbourne seems a woman determined that no detail should escape her careful orchestration."

Eleanor arched a brow. "You disapprove?"

"On the contrary." He set his glass upon the table. "I find it rather admirable. Precision is a most underestimated quality."

She chewed her lip, intrigued. "And do you yourself possess such a virtue, Mr Blackwood?"

He let out a soft laugh, the sound warm and rich, much like the wine in his glass. "I fear I am rather more inclined towards instinct than precision." He paused, regarding her with a thoughtful expression. "And you, Miss Carstone? What are you more inclined to, logic or impulse?"

She considered him for a moment before replying, "I should like to say logic, but I fear impulse has led me astray on more than one occasion."

"Then we are alike in that respect."

There was something in his tone—an unspoken thread of understanding—that sent a shiver of awareness through her. She found herself uncharacteristically affected by his presence, by the quiet confidence in his gaze, the effortless charm that wove through his words. It was a dangerous thing, she realised, to find oneself intrigued by a man who she would never see again beyond this weekend.

Before she could reply, the next course arrived. A boar's head, its snout adorned with a sprig of rosemary, was carried forth to much praise.

Conversation turned to merriment, with laughter punctuating the clink of silver upon porcelain. Attendees leaned close to one another, sharing speculations about the murder mystery, each eager to prove their own superiority in deduction.

Eleanor noticed how throughout the meal guests formed alliances, drawn together by familiarity or the ease of existing friendships.

Attending an event like this alone meant stepping into a world already in motion—where glances skimmed past her in search of a familiar face and conversations folded in on themselves, leaving her at the edges. The sensation of being an outsider was nothing new to her, nor did it unsettle her—but the quiet, human urge to belong lingered all the same.

Solitude had never been unwelcome, yet the theatrics of the weekend—the shared intrigue, the hushed conspiracies—threw it into sharper relief, leaving her in an unfamiliar place.

She, however, was acutely aware of Nathaniel's presence beside her. The way his sleeve brushed hers when he reached for his wine, the way his fingers lingered against the stem of his glass as he considered his words. Without explanation, she found herself drawn to the stranger as strongly as seas are drawn to the moon.

The last course arrived—a towering trifle laced with brandy, its layers of sponge, custard, and cream gleaming in the candlelight. Not everyone left enough space for the pièce de résistance!

Once the staff had cleared the last plates and refilled the glasses for a final toast, Mrs Winterbourne stood with effortless poise. The table fell silent, all eyes turning to their hostess.

"I do hope," she said, her voice carrying the soft authority of one accustomed to command, "that you have all enjoyed this evening's repast."

A murmur of assent followed with enthusiastic nods and exclamations of appreciation.

"I must confess," she continued, a knowing smile playing at her lips, "that I had a particular reason for ensuring you were all most attentive throughout the meal."

There was a slight pause, the anticipation palpable. "For you see, the next clue was in plain sight all this evening. I do hope you are observant people."

A ripple of eagerness spread through the room, attendees exchanging glances, their minds racing through the details of the meal. Eleanor's own thoughts whirled as she mentally retraced every element of the dinner—the food, the decorations, the conversation. What had been hidden in plain sight?

Nathaniel leaned close to her side, his voice a low murmur meant for her ears alone. "Well, Miss Carstone, shall we see if our combined intellects are equal to the task?"

She met his gaze. "Indeed, Mr Blackwood." Enjoying both the continued Austen role-playing, and the sparkle in his eyes, a slow smile curved her lips. "Let us see if we cannot outwit our competition."

*****

As the plates were cleared, the dining room hummed with the pleasant din of conversation. Eleanor stayed seated beside Nathaniel, both their minds preoccupied with the mystery laid before them. Mrs Winterbourne's words still lingered in the air, tantalising and evasive—what clue had been presented to them throughout the meal?

28

Nathaniel inched his chair closer. "We must consider the evening with a keen eye. Every detail may hold significance."

Eleanor nodded. "Indeed. The question is, was it in the food, the decorations, or something else?"

They had little time to reflect before everyone began to rise from the table, many moving in pairs or small groups, murmuring theories and speculation.

The open doors of the Bluebell Parlour invited them in to participate in after-dinner drinks.

A tribute to the woodland glades beyond the hall where the flowers bloomed in abundance each spring, painted bluebells wound their way across the pale green walls. The delicate blossoms twined through carved wood panels and adorned the fine china on the sideboard, lending the room an air of quiet charm.

Though this evening, no such peace could be found. A lively discussion soon took root, voices rising and falling as arguments were made and dismissed with equal fervour.

Others drifted over to the card tables, shuffling gilt-edged decks with idle hands while their thoughts remained fixed upon the evening's intrigue.

Near the hearth, a knot of people debated in hushed tones, their expressions grave as they weighed each suspicion with the solemnity of a judge at the assizes. A few, feigning disinterest, positioned themselves by the pianoforte, though the melody they coaxed from its keys was halting, their minds plainly elsewhere.

Eleanor and Nathaniel lingered at the threshold, the movement of the room unfolding before them like a well-rehearsed tableau. Somewhere amidst the hum of voices and rustle of silk, the truth lay hidden.

"I propose," Nathaniel said, offering his arm, "that we retreat to someplace a little quieter where we can examine our thoughts in comfort."

Eleanor hesitated only a moment before taking it, aware of the heat of his arm beneath the crisp sleeve of his evening jacket. "You mean without listening ears!"

Nathaniel glanced down at her, a half-smile playing at his lips. "I find, Miss Carstone, that one is far more at liberty to speak one's mind when not surrounded by an audience eager to misinterpret every word."

After looking in both the morning room and the library and finding them occupied, Nathaniel led Eleanor down the corridor to the cordoned-off Winter Room. He lifted the purple cord and indicated that she should enter.

Eleanor glanced both ways down and up the corridor. "But we've been asked to stay out of these rooms."

"I won't tell if you don't." He raised his eyebrows in question.

With another quick check both ways, Eleanor hurried into the dark room.

The Winter Room, though grand, had an air of intimacy about it, its once-elegant furnishings draped in dust sheets, the carved mantelpiece dull with neglect. No fire had been laid, and the air held the chill of long disuse. A heavy silence pressed upon them, broken only by the faint creak of the floorboards as Nathaniel stepped further inside.

Eleanor trailed a gloved hand along the back of an armchair, tracing the rough weave of the fabric beneath her fingers. "It must have been beautiful once."

Nathaniel reached for a candle from a nearby sideboard and struck a match. The weak glow did little to dispel the gloom, but it was enough to cast flickering shadows against the faded wallpaper. "A fitting place for secrets."

Eleanor turned to him, the dim light sharpening the angles of his face. "Then let us uncover one. What do we know?"

Nathaniel gestured for her to sit, then took his place beside her on top of the dust sheet, elbows resting upon his knees. "Let us think logically. What was presented before us tonight that was unusual?"

Eleanor furrowed her brow. "The meal was in keeping with the period—though some of the dishes were rather more modern."

"But not really a clue."

She drummed her fingers against her lap. "Then there was the boar's head."

Nathaniel nodded. "A fine centrepiece, but it cannot be so simple. It must be something more subtle."

They sat in silence for a moment, both reviewing the evening's proceedings in their minds. Then Eleanor's eyes widened.

"The Christmas presents," she said.

Nathaniel straightened. "Maybes."

Eleanor reached into the pocket of her gown and drew forth the tiny package she had been given, still neatly sealed. She turned it over in her hands before tugging at the ribbon and unfolding the paper. Inside was a small, round chocolate truffle, which she popped into her mouth. "Mmm, coffee and cream."

Beside her, Nathaniel unwrapped his own, examining the contents before offering her the truffle with a slight smirk. "I suspect you might appreciate this more than me."

She accepted it with a grin, then checked the tiny box, pulling out a folded slip of parchment.

Her heart quickened as she opened it. A bubble of childlike excitement made her grin.

There, in delicate script, were a few words:

Find the next envelope where the nightingale sings.

She looked up to find Nathaniel watching her, his gaze keen. "I rather think we are one step closer," he said.

Eleanor read the clue aloud before glancing around the room. "The nightingale... That must be a reference to something within the house."

Nathaniel stood, offering his hand to her. "Let us see if we can uncover it before the others."

After blowing out the candle and checking the coast was clear, they moved into the hall, where another grand Christmas tree stood in all its splendour, its Victorian ornaments glinting in the candlelight. Beyond it, the house stretched into corridors filled with fine paintings and antique furnishings, each holding the quiet history of Winterbourne Hall.

They searched methodically, their conversation a quiet exchange of deductions. With each passing moment, they grew more attuned to each other's thoughts, working in silent synchrony.

At last, in a small parlour at the far end of the house, Eleanor spotted it. A delicate porcelain nightingale perched upon a side table, its painted feathers so lifelike it seemed poised to take flight. Beneath it, half-tucked beneath the base, was an envelope made of the finest cream paper. Its texture bore the slight roughness of hand-pressed vellum.

Embossed at the centre of the flap, in deep cerulean wax, was the Winterbourne crest—a proud stag beneath a canopy of oak leaves, its noble form captured in exquisite detail. The seal had been broken, meaning someone else had found it before them.

Nathaniel pulled out a slip of paper and read aloud, "Among you are six players. three hold secrets, two a motive, and one of them the weapon. Discover their faces, and you shall find the reason for murder."

Eleanor took the pencil out and opened her notebook. "Six players… the actors among us."

Nathaniel nodded. "It is rather clever, is it not? We must determine which of our guests are part of the performance." He tucked the paper back inside the envelope and replaced it under the bird.

They returned to the main hall, where a number of people made their farewells, bundling into taxis or stepping into the horse-drawn carriage Mrs Winterbourne had so generously hired for those staying at The Willow & Rose Hotel in Willowcombe Village.

Eleanor turned to Nathaniel. "We should make note of who remains. From them, we shall find our six actors."

He smiled. "And from them, our killer. Though throwing us off guard, she might have paid for some of the actors to stay at the hotel in the village."

"Oh, true."

A thrill coursed through Eleanor's veins—not only at the mystery itself, but at the way Nathaniel's eyes lingered on hers, as though they shared some unspoken understanding beyond the confines of the game.

With that, they bid their final goodnights to those departing and made their way to the guest rooms upstairs. The electric candle sconces lit the corridors, whispering with the hush of an old house settling into night.

As Eleanor reached her door, she turned once more to Nathaniel.

"We shall reconvene in the morning," he said, inclining his head. "Though I daresay, Miss Eleanor, that you will not rest until you have pieced together every fragment of this puzzle."

She smiled. "And neither, I suspect, will you."

With that, she stepped inside, closing the door behind her with care, her mind alive with possibilities.

*****

After washing and changing into her warm pyjamas, Eleanor settled into the plush armchair by the window, the house around her now hushed and still, she let her mind drift once more to Mrs Winterbourne's words.

The presents. It had been far too obvious. If Mrs Winterbourne wished to test their ingenuity, would she have placed such a blatant clue before them? No, there had to be something more—something cleverly concealed beneath the surface, waiting for those with sharper wits to uncover.

Reaching for her notebook, she flipped to a fresh page and began to list the guests she could remember.

Mr and Mrs Dunlop – elderly, don't appear to be actors
The Leighton sisters – too keen to solve the puzzle, not actors

Adam & Beryl Beauchamp – ?
Mr and Mrs Fairfax – ?
Leo Vaunt – ?

Her brow furrowed as she examined them, the Regency-styled, low-wattage, standard lamp cast a soft shadow across the page. Names held power; names could hide secrets.

And then, as her pencil hovered over the last name, realisation struck her like a sudden gust of wind.

Leo Vaunt.

She rolled his name under her breath, her heart quickening. It was not a name at all—it was an anagram. Although one 'v' was missing, rearranged, the letters formed vol-au-vent—one of the more modern dishes served at dinner. A slow smile curled upon her lips.

Leo Vaunt must be one of the actors!

The thrill of discovery banished any notion of sleep. If there was one, there could be more.

She rose, slipping on her dressing gown before easing the door open, wincing as the hinges creaked in protest. The corridor stood in shadows by the turn-downed lights, and the great house groaned in the night, as all old houses do, whispering to those who care to listen.

Eleanor moved down the staircase, her slippers muffled silent against the well-cushioned carpets beneath her toes. Her breath came shallow as she reached the reception hall.

The guest book had been left open on the grand mahogany counter, precisely as though it were meant to be examined. The fire in the adjacent parlour had burned low, its embers pulsing like the heartbeat of the house.

She hesitated, listening. No sound but the distant tick of a grandfather clock and the occasional moan of wind against the tall windows.

After setting aside the quill that had been carelessly left on the pages of the book, she ran her fingers down the list of names, searching each one intently before hastily copying them into her notebook.

And then—there it was. Another name that sent a spark of recognition through her mind.

Sally Montray had signed in as Sal Mon. She pressed a hand to her lips, stifling an exclamation. Salmon—another modern dish from their meal.

Two actors revealed.

Her pulse thrummed with exhilaration. Whoever had devised this mystery had done so with a keen intellect, concealing clues beneath the fabric of the evening's festivities.

Not wanting it to remain an obvious clue, she closed the guest book and put it on a shelf below the counter. Grinning at her mischief she turned, preparing to retreat to her chamber. But as she did so, a sudden draught came from nowhere and whirled around, causing her to shiver. A shadow, cast long against the wall, moved in a way that did not belong to her.

Eleanor froze, her breath catching in her throat.

Someone was awake.

And someone had been watching.

Chapter 3

ELEANOR AWOKE TO the pale light of morning filtering through the heavy drapes, illuminating the frost-laced windowpanes. After getting up and dressed, she stretched languidly, relieved to wear her well-worn jeans and a delicate cashmere jumper, leaving the confines of a corseted gown for later. The thought of not being trussed up in Regency finery until the evening's festivities was a small mercy, indeed.

After lacing up her boots, she wandered over to the window, pushing aside the thick curtain to take in the view of Winterbourne Hall's sprawling estate. In its prime, it must have been a vision of aristocratic glory, with manicured gardens, well-tended hedgerows, and elegant stone walls marking the boundaries of its domain.

Now, the grounds bore the signs of both time's decay and a determined effort to restore them. Overgrown pathways had been partially cleared, offering glimpses of the estate's former splendour, while along the kitchen garden's perimeter, workers carefully rebuilt the crumbling stone wall. Life was returning to Winterbourne—slowly, steadily—its faded glory stirring once more. Eleanor found herself captivated by the quiet resilience of the place.

She descended the grand staircase and entered the breakfast room, where the golden glow of the fire lent a welcome warmth against the crisp morning air. And there, seated with an air of quiet authority, was Nathaniel. He beckoned her to his table.

At the sight of him, unfamiliar warmth curled in her stomach. She had noted last night that he was handsome—in a quiet, unassuming sort of way. Not the kind of man whose looks turned heads the moment he entered a room, but rather one whose appeal deepened upon closer study. There was intelligence in his gaze, a steadiness in his manner, and a touch of warmth about his smile that rendered him all the more agreeable upon further acquaintance.

This morning, in the bright light of day, she found herself lingering a fraction too long on the precise curve of his lips, their shape undeniably designed to invite a kiss. His expression, a mixture of mischief and knowingness, suggested that her lapse had not gone unnoticed.

"Good morning, Miss Carstone," he said, setting down his teacup with an elegant motion. "I trust you slept well?"

"Quite well, thank you," she replied, fidgeting with her hands while trying to school her features into composure. "And yourself?"

"Exceedingly so, though I confess, I half expected an illicit midnight excursion, given your keen investigative nature. But alas, the furtive knock on my door to invite me on a clandestine exploration never materialised."

"Well, as it happens…"

"Please, do sit down and join me for breakfast. I am getting rather a creak in the neck."

Longing to share her late-night discovery, she pulled out a chair and slid into it.

Her haste caused him to grin even more. "Hungry, Miss Carstone?"

She chuckled and locked onto his perfect cobalt eyes. "I think when we are not in costume we should drop the formalities, don't you? Please call me Eleanor."

"You might want to sit back."

"Pardon?"

Nathaniel nodded to her side where a member of staff, dressed in Regency costume stood with a tray.

Eleanor leaned back and smiled as the footman placed a steaming bowl of porridge before her. "Coffee or tea, my lady?"

Being called a lady brought a playful grin to her lips. "Coffee please."

Nathaniel chuckled, selecting a ripe fig from the fruit platter between them. "Personally, I need at least three cups of coffee before my brain kicks into gear. Thankfully, they serve jolly good filter coffee here. Now, enlighten me as to what you have uncovered? That's what you were going to say isn't it? That you've worked out another clue."

She recounted her late-night revelation regarding the anagrammed names, watching as his eyes gleamed with interest. "I have managed to uncover two of the actors—one whose name was an anagram of vol-au-vent, and another one who signed the guest book as Sal Mon."

"Ingenious, I love it! Food related villains. May I take a look at the names you jotted down?"

Nathaniel studied the list with his lips twisting with concentration. After a few moments, he looked up and smiled. "You missed one." He tapped a finger triumphantly against a particular entry. "Think about the syllables, Miss Angela Pellidoc—you can rearrange them to make capelli d'angelo."

She peered closer, her mind racing to piece together the puzzle. When the answer struck, she half-suppressed a laugh and shook her head. "Of course, Angel Hair! I thought that bowl out of place with everything else they served. That brings us to three of our six players."

"Which means… we are halfway to unravelling the murder suspects. An encouraging start, if I may say so."

In a conspiratorial manner, he put his elbow on the table and leaned forward. In a hushed tone, "If you had to guess, what motive would you think the suspects have to murder the stunning Lady Genevieve?"

"You think she's beautiful?" Heat instantly flamed her cheeks as she realised the silliness of her question.

With a far too wide grin, he leaned back. "Despite the fake blood soaking the back of her head, I found her delicate, umm, porcelain-like."

"And you find that attractive?" Baffled, Eleanor couldn't help the sharpness that edged her words. What was wrong with her? Why should she care? But the knowledge that she was maybe the complete opposite of breakable told her that this rather dashing man would never find her attractive.

"There is something about a woman who cries 'take care of me' that appeals to me." Noticing red flaming Eleanor's cheeks and neck he rushed to add, "Please don't get all women's lib on me, I also like clever, strong-minded women. We are all different, are we not?"

Wanting to change the subject she went back to his question. "The same reasons motivate most murders: jealousy, revenge, anger, fear, and greed. I shouldn't imagine that a game will go beyond the obvious."

"So we need to discover what reason each of our suspect might have."

Eleanor studied him for a moment. "I asked you last night what it is you do, and I don't think you properly answered me." Picking up her spoon she tucked into the creamy porridge before it went cold.

Nathaniel hesitated for the briefest moment before he smiled and leaned back in his chair. "A writer. I find places such as these…" he waved his arm to take in their surroundings, "are excellent sources of inspiration. Something about their history, their secrets buried beneath layers of dust and time—it all makes for a rather compelling backdrop."

She arched an eyebrow, sensing there was more he was not saying, but let it pass for the time being. "A writer," she mused. "How fascinating."

"And you?"

Crossing her fingers under the table. "I am a museum curator. I've taken December off to visit as many historical estates in Devon as I can. This place captivated me more than most. Which is why I'm determined to win the prize—staying here another week would be nothing short of a dream."

Nathaniel regarded her with something like admiration. "Then I shall do my utmost to ensure your success, Eleanor. We shall not let that prize slip through your fingers."

Somewhat surprised by his ready offer of assistance, she found herself smiling. The sound of her name on his lips had warmed her cockles—as her gran would have said. "Alright, let us see if two heads are indeed better than one."

*****

With their morning meal finished and their theories stacking up like well-placed chess pieces, Eleanor and Nathaniel set about their next task—discreetly interrogating their three identified actors. If they were to solve this mystery and claim the coveted prize, they needed to uncover not only the motive but which of these hired players had committed the fictitious crime.

They found their first suspect, Sally, in the drawing room, sipping tea by the window. A striking woman in her early fifties, she dressed with understated sophistication in a blue, soft-fabric

41

suit, and held herself with the poise of someone accustomed to admiration.

Nathaniel approached first, settling into an armchair opposite her while Eleanor perched on the edge of a nearby chaise lounge. "Good morning," he greeted with an easy smile. "I hope you don't mind, but Eleanor and I were hoping to pick your brain a little. You see, we're quite invested in getting to the bottom of last night's terrible crime."

Sally gave a knowing smile, swirling her tea before taking a delicate sip. "Ah, Lady Genevieve's unfortunate demise. Tragic. And what would you like to know?"

Eleanor leaned forward. "For starters, how did you know her?"

Sally's expression remained fixed, but Eleanor caught the subtle way her fingers tightened around her teacup. "I knew her well enough, our paths crossed a few times."

Nathaniel arched an eyebrow. "In what capacity?"

Sally let out a soft, theatrical laugh. "Let's just say she and I were interested in the same... things. But, darling, we didn't exactly see eye to eye. She had a rather nasty habit of undercutting those she saw as competition."

Eleanor exchanged a glance with Nathaniel. "Competition?"

Sally exhaled with all the flair of Orsino in the throes of longing. "The woman had a habit of taking everything she wanted. She had influence, and she wasn't afraid to wield it. There are whispers, of course... that she didn't always play fair." She gave them both a knowing look. "Some might even say she was the sort of woman who made enemies wherever she went."

"And were you one of those enemies?" Nathaniel asked.

Sally's lips curled into a smile. "If I were, darling, would I admit it?"

Eleanor smiled back. "Probably not. Can I ask… what do you do for a living?"

"I'm a novelist, though I would rather you refrained from sharing that information." Sally cast a quick glance around, as if to ensure no one else was listening.

Eleanor's interest piqued. "Why ever not? That is a most admirable profession."

Sally let out a soft chuckle. "Admirable, perhaps. But respectable—not for a woman. I write under a man's name. It affords me a freedom I would not otherwise enjoy."

Eleanor tilted her head. "But surely, such pretences are unnecessary?"

Sally gave a knowing look. "You would think so, but publishers—readers, even—still favour a man's hand for certain kinds of stories. A lady scribbling away in a parlour is acceptable, provided she confines herself to sentimental tales. Anything more daring, and well… the world is not quite as modern as it likes to pretend."

"That seems most unfair."

"Unfair, yes, but not unfamiliar." Sally shrugged. "I've had to start over once before, and I daresay I will again if circumstances demand it. It is an unfortunate thing when the wrong person takes offence at your success."

A flicker of something unreadable crossed Sally's face. Eleanor hesitated. "What happened?"

Sally's smile lacked warmth. "Let us just say that not all wounds are visible, and not all battles are fought with swords."

She wanted to press further, but Sally raised a hand. "Besides, I rather like my new name. S. W. Samuel turned out to be more fortunate than Sally ever was."

Eleanor wrote it down, then looked up quickly, hoping to catch Sally off guard. "Where were you when she was murdered?"

Sally set down her teacup with a quiet clink. "Darling, were we not all together in one room? The entire party was present when Mrs Winterbourne made her speech."

Nathaniel tapped a finger against his knee. "Every single person?"

Sally's expression turned mischievous. "Ah. Now that you mention it… I did spot Leo Vaunt slipping away for at least ten minutes during the speech." She sighed for good measure. "I assumed he was off brooding or powdering his nose, but who knows? *Perhaps...* he had something rather more sinister in mind."

Eleanor made another note in her book. They thanked Sally for her time, then made their way to the library.

*****

Their second suspect, Angela Pellidoc, was reclining on a velvet settee in the library. She was a woman in her early forties with sleek, chestnut-brown hair cut in a chic, shoulder-length bob and the sharp, assessing gaze of someone who missed little. She greeted them with a cool smile as they approached.

Nathaniel extended his hand. "Good morning, Mrs Pellidoc. Would you mind if we asked you a few questions?"

"I am *Ms*, if you don't mind." She waved at them to sit on the chairs opposite her. "You're an inquisitive pair, aren't you?"

she said, tilting her head. "I do admire a bit of enthusiasm. Though, do be careful—it wouldn't do to get too close to the truth too soon."

Eleanor folded her arms. "And why is that?"

Angela traced the rim of her teacup with one perfectly manicured nail. "Because in any good mystery, those who dig too deep sometimes find themselves in over their heads."

Nathaniel smirked. "Is that a threat?"

"A caution," Angela corrected. "Lady Genevieve was not a woman to be trifled with. She was… difficult. But there are those who still might not appreciate their secrets being exposed."

Eleanor sensed there was more Angela wasn't saying. "How did you know her?"

"Oh, she and I had a rather complicated history. Let's say she had a way of making sure she remained centre stage at all times. Some found it endearing; others, exhausting."

Nathaniel leaned in. "And which were you?"

Angela's lips curved into a secretive smile. "Somewhere in between."

Before Eleanor could press further, Angela gave a thoughtful hum. "I will say, though, I'm rather surprised at how composed Sally Monterey is. Considering."

Eleanor raised an eyebrow. "Considering what?"

Angela gave a little shrug. "Oh, just that Lady Genevieve ruined her career."

A pointed glance passed between Nathaniel and Eleanor. Sally had only that Genevieve had wanted something of hers, but Angela had handed them something far more damning.

"Did she now?" Nathaniel mused. "That's interesting."

Angela smiled serenely. "Isn't it just?"

They thanked her for her time and made their way to the parlour.

*****

They found their last food related suspect, Leo Vaunt, lounging in the parlour, reading a newspaper. He was a dapper man in his fifties with a well-groomed beard and an air of practised ease.

"You have come to interrogate me, I see." He set aside his reading. "Quite the detectives, aren't you? I will let you into a secret… you are the first to question me. Jolly good work."

Eleanor smiled. "Thank you. Would you tell us about Genevieve, please?"

Leo sighed with a heavy puff. "Lady Genevieve had a talent for making herself indispensable—until she wasn't. She knew things about people. And sometimes, that knowledge put her at risk."

"Are you saying someone had a reason to silence her?" Nathaniel asked.

Leo tapped his nose conspiratorially. "I'm saying, in life, one should be careful about the enemies they make."

Eleanor took the seat opposite him and tapped on her notepad. "Sally Monterey mentioned that you disappeared for about ten minutes last night. What were you doing?"

Leo's mouth twitched. "Oh, is that what she said? Convenient. And did she also mention that she had plenty of motive herself?"

Eleanor and Nathaniel exchanged a glance.

46

Leo leaned back with an amused expression. "Ask yourself, if Lady Genevieve had been responsible for someone's career crumbling to dust... wouldn't they want a little revenge?"

Eleanor noted that he hadn't denied slipping away. Another intriguing puzzle piece. "And how exactly did she do that?"

Leo licked his lips in anticipation of spilling gossip. "Genevieve took a fancy to Peter Browning, Sally's agent, but Peter had what we shall call... a *soft spot* for Sally. Genevieve, in a fit of spite, spread a false rumour stating Sally had plagiarised another author's work."

"But she hadn't," said Nathaniel.

"Certainly not. The whole thing was a lie to ruin Sally. Very nearly did as the *love-struck* Peter decided to drop her."

"What a terrible thing to do," Eleanor said.

"Don't judge the dead too harshly, the poor woman might have been a tad mean to be sure, but beneath it all... a woman desperate to be loved."

They thanked him and made to leave, but hushed voices drifted in from the hallway and made them pause.

"I've figured one of them out," one of the voices said triumphantly.

"How?" the other whispered back.

"Simple. When they were discussing last night's events, they slipped and said 'my character' instead of 'my role.' Dead giveaway."

"Who was it?"

In the quietest whisper, "Albert..."

The voice dropped so low that Eleanor and Nathaniel didn't catch the surname. They exchanged a look, another name to their list.

The dining room at Winterbourne Hall, though somewhat faded with time, held an air of quiet opulence. The long table, set with silverware that had seen better days, was lined with guests who, for the most part, were more interested in speculation than their plates. Mrs Winterbourne, seated at the head, presided over the gathering with the satisfaction of one who had orchestrated a most diverting entertainment.

Eleanor took her seat for lunch beside Nathaniel, keenly aware of the quiet confidence in his manner. Though not a word had been spoken on the matter, they had fallen into the habit of sitting together, as though drawn by some unspoken accord. Amongst attendees composed chiefly of married couples, it was natural, perhaps, that two solitary figures should gravitate towards one another. And yet, Eleanor could not suppress the quiet hope that their inclination to do so stemmed from something more than mere circumstance.

"My dear friends," said Mrs Winterbourne in a commanding tone, her gaze sweeping the table. "It appears a few things have gone missing. A limited edition of *Northanger Abbey* from the library, a humidor that belonged to my great-grandfather from the study, and the guest book from the lobby."

Eleanor nearly choked, and Nathaniel, ever composed, was swift to pass her a glass of water.

When at last she had recovered, Mrs Winterbourne resumed, her voice measured but firm. "I assume these items have simply been misplaced and trust they will be returned forthwith. On another matter, might I entreat whoever persists in rearranging the furniture in the study to desist?" A slow, surveying glance silenced the murmurs that had begun to ripple through the company, but no one stepped forward to confess.

Across the table, Angela Pellidoc stirred her soup with languid indifference, the pearls at her throat catching the pale winter sunlight that streamed through the tall, paned windows. "It is a rather fine thing, is it not?" she mused, glancing up. "A house brimming with intrigue. One might almost believe the ghosts of its former occupants linger still."

"Or at least, someone wants us to believe it," Nathaniel said under his breath, with a glance at Eleanor.

Before she could reply, a shriek rang through the room, the high-pitched kind that silenced all conversation. Every head turned towards Mrs Sophia De'Luciosi, whose wavering hand pointed to her cutlery. "My spoon!" she cried, her voice trembling. "There is blood on my spoon!"

Silence fell, broken only by the scrape of chairs as the guests leaned forward. Eleanor caught sight of the offending utensil, the spoon tainted with something dark. The servants exchanged glances, none moving to take it.

"It must be a jest," Sally Monterey said with a flap of her hand.

"Or a warning." Leo knocked back his wine.

Mrs Winterbourne, never one to let hysteria reign in her house, lifted a brow. "There is no cause for alarm. I daresay it is no more than an unfortunate accident. The matter will be looked into." She flapped at a server to clear it away. "Now, let us not allow such unpleasantness to ruin our meal."

Leo Vaunt set down his spoon with deliberate care. "An unfortunate accident, indeed," he said, his tone light but his eyes sharp. "Though I cannot help but observe that misfortunes seem to multiply in this house. First, Lady Genevieve, a curious series of disappearances, and now this."

Sally Monterey gave a short, mirthless laugh. "Curious, yes, though I suspect some know more than they claim." She leaned back, fingers tapping idly against the stem of her wine glass. "It is strange, is it not, Mr Vaunt, that you arrived here with barely a history to speak of, and yet you seem so remarkably well-opined?"

Leo's smile did not reach his eyes. "My dear Miss Monterey, if we are to discuss mysterious pasts, shall we begin with your own? Or would that be an inconvenient detour?"

Sally's grip on her glass tightened. "Say what you mean, sir, and spare us the theatrics."

"I simply note that a lady of your profession would possess a keen understanding of people—their motives, their weaknesses. An author must be a master of observation, must they not? Skilled in guiding a reader's attention, in shaping perception, and even in misdirection when the tale requires it. A most useful talent, I imagine, should one have something to conceal."

Sally's lips parted as though she might deliver a scathing retort, but instead, she smiled—a slow, knowing smile that sent a ripple of unease through the table. "Well, well. It seems we are both rather adept at that, are we not?"

A charged silence followed. Somewhere in the distance, the grandfather clock in the hall struck one, its chime reverberating through the quiet.

Nathaniel had been watching with keen interest. "I cannot decide whether they wish to marry or murder each other."

Eleanor hid her mirth behind her napkin. "Perhaps both."

Mrs Winterbourne cleared her throat, drawing the attention back to herself with practised ease. "Now that we have entertained ourselves with this lively exchange, might we return to our luncheon?"

A few nervous chuckles followed, but as the meal resumed, a sense of unease lingered in the air. Eleanor met Nathaniel's gaze, his expression one of quiet amusement.

"Do you suppose that we are being taunted?"

"That depends on whether we are the ones meant to be afraid."

Smiling, he considered her for a moment. "I find it rather delightful that you refuse to be cowed by theatrics."

She put her head back and grinned, half-smiling at the game and half at the sheer joy of knowing the man next to her liked her company. "I daresay I have yet to encounter theatrics capable of unsettling me. Besides, though I have to keep reminding myself, we are, after all, only playing a game."

The skin around his eyes crinkled. "You have the most admirable traits."

"Do you think that conversation was designed to sweep the bloodied spoon issue under the carpet?"

"That is quite possible."

The light lunch of soup and a platter of cheeses continued, and through it all Eleanor remained keenly aware of Nathaniel beside her, the warmth of his presence, the occasional brush of his sleeve against hers. When he leaned in once more, voice low, it was not speculation that he offered, but something softer.

"I hope you do not find my company wearisome."

She glanced at him, eyes bright. "Not in the least."

A small smile touched his lips. "Then I count myself fortunate."

Eleanor wondered at the ease with which he remained in character and whether he would be bold enough to say such things outside of a historical drama.

Across the table, Mrs De'Luciosi shuddered, pushing her untouched soup bowl with distrust. "If this is how lunch proceeds. I dread to think what dinner will bring."

Chapter 4

WHEN LUNCHEON CONCLUDED, Eleanor went to the ballroom. The house had grown quiet, save for the distant strains of conversation from the parlour and the occasional footstep echoing through the hallways. Somewhere, Nathaniel had taken to the grounds, no doubt seeking the solace of the crisp winter air. But Eleanor found herself drawn once more to the glass display case where the fabled glass ball rested upon its velvet stand.

Mrs Winterbourne entered the room with the measured grace of one long accustomed to the presence of fine things. She paused at Eleanor's side, regarding the bauble with an air of wistfulness.

"It is beautiful, is it not?" she sighed, folding her hands before her.

"Exceedingly so," Eleanor replied, leaning in to study the delicate golden filigree entwining the glass, the mistletoe stems twisting together in intricate, fragile detail. "But its true wonder lies in its history."

Beatrice smiled. "Ah, so you know where it comes from. You do have the heart of a scholar. Most admire it for its beauty alone, yet you have sought out the story beneath. Do you know the legend surrounding it, Miss Carstone?"

"Please, call me Eleanor."

"Very well, and you must call me Beatrice—when we are not *in* the game. In that, staff and guests are requested to call me by my surname. But you," she playfully tapped Eleanor's arm with a finger, "may call me by my first name at moments such as this, as all my friends do."

Eleanor smiled and then gestured at the locked cabinet. "I understand the set comprised of five, made at the behest of Prince Albert for the Queen. But what became of the others?"

"Ah." Beatrice's expression grew distant. "After Her Majesty's passing, the baubles were given to a dear friend of hers who had always admired them. From there, their fate became something of a mystery and myths and legends began to abound. This one, at least, found its way back to my family."

Eleanor turned to her with interest. "You mean it was yours before?"

Beatrice nodded. "My grandmother was gifted it many years ago, but my father, in difficult times, was forced to sell it. I had long believed it lost until, by sheer happenstance, my husband came upon a man who claimed to possess it. Jonathan, on a whim, paid a rather alarming sum to restore it to me on our anniversary. The man had always been an enigma to me. So strict and abrupt, and then like this… granting me unbelievable joy. It is a shame that his love for me went no further than duty. We had such a bitter end."

"Oh, I'm so sorry to hear that."

Beatrice straightened and shook her shoulders. A good head shorter than Eleanor and slight in build, she suddenly seemed (despite the many layered Regency dress) a fragile woman and Eleanor became overwhelmed with a longing to help shoulder her problems.

"Water under the bridge and all that," Beatrice said her face aglow with resolution.

Eleanor regarded the bauble with renewed reverence, wondering how it had arrived in the Winterbourne household in the first place. Her fingers itched to open it, to unfurl the delicate gold key nestled within. "The engraving on the key, was that the Prince's own design?"

"Kitching & Abud made them, but yes, it is believed that Albert told them exactly what he wanted." Beatrice smiled her past woes slipping away. "Indeed. Each bauble encases a key, and upon each one is inscribed a single phrase—an intimate message from Albert to Victoria." She paused, lowering her voice as though to preserve the romance of it. "Ours bears the words 'Dein auf ewig, Albert.'"

Eleanor traced the words in her mind, the same inscription she had read countless times in the dossier upstairs: Yours forever, Albert. A simple sentiment, yet profound—the kind of devotion that endured beyond even the longest of reigns.

"It is only fiction, you know."

"What is?" Eleanor asked, glancing up.

"The myth that possessing all five keys will unlock a hidden treasure."

Eleanor allowed herself a small smile. "I reached the same conclusion. After all, what use are keys without something to unlock? I prefer to think Albert intended them as a symbol— that he had, in truth, unlocked Victoria's heart."

"Precisely! You are well-informed." Beatrice regarded her with an appraising look, one brow arched.

"It is my profession to uncover truth where it is obscured. In my pursuit of the remarkable, I came across a study on the baubles, compiled by Professor Reginald Arluke."

"I have read that myself." Beatrice nodded thoughtfully. "Full of fascinating details, but what touched me most was the photograph of Albert and Victoria standing before their Christmas tree, his gifts displayed on the tree behind them. My great-grandparents imitated that pose, you know—stood before their own tree, the bauble prominently displayed. I never realised they were recreating the royal photograph until I came across it in the professor's journal."

"You have an old photograph with the bauble in it?"

"Yes, framed on the pianoforte in the morning room. Do have a look next time you are in there."

"I shall."

Beatrice sighed. "I often wonder where the other baubles are now, and whether their keys still carry their whispers of love." She turned to Eleanor with a considered look. "I hope that when you depart Winterbourne Hall, you shall take some small part of its history with you."

Eleanor met her gaze, the burden of the mission settled over her. "I daresay I already have. Beatrice, I have something to confess."

A light sparked in the matriarch's eyes. "What is that, dear?"

About to blurt out why she had come to the Hall, something caught in her chest warning her to silence. "I moved the guest book. Only to the shelf behind the counter though, it should be easy to find."

"The staff have searched high and low for it, it is not to be found anywhere."

"Oh!"

"Yes, oh, indeed. Obviously one of guests does not believe in playing fair and took it to stop other players learning who the suspects are."

Eleanor went bright red. "It wasn't me, I assure you."

"I am most glad to hear it. Now I must do the rounds and ensure everyone is enjoying themselves." Beatrice smiled and left Eleanor to continue her admiration, a swish of skirts and a lingering smell of delicate rose and the hostess was gone.

With a reluctant hand, Eleanor pulled her mobile phone out of her back jean pocket and began a series of photographs, catching the bauble from as many angles as possible. As she slipped the phone back into her pocket, she was sure of one thing—Mrs Winterbourne had no idea the item might have been stolen by the man who sold it to her husband.

*****

The grandfather clock in the hallway struck three, each deliberate chime reverberating through the house. Descending the staircase, Eleanor found Nathaniel already waiting, one hand resting against the carved banister, his gaze fixed upon some distant thought. At the sight of her, his expression sharpened into awareness.

"You are most punctual," he said.

"And you likewise. Where shall we go first?"

"Mrs De'Luciosi provided quite the spectacle at luncheon. The bloodied spoon, I suspect, was intended to elicit a reaction, and hers was so exaggerated as to render it almost laughable."

Eleanor inclined her head. "Sally called it a warning, which implies foreknowledge. Sophia De'Luciosi must be part of the acting troupe."

"A conclusion I had reached myself. Shall we?" He indicated the path ahead.

Smiling, she fell into step beside him. "Where are we bound?"

"I happened to overhear her mention a fondness for reading amongst the Bougainvillea and Hoyas."

Eleanor cast him a knowing glance. "Happened to overhear?"

"Miss Carstone, whatever are you implying?"

Before she could reply, the library door swung open, and Mr and Mrs Dunlop emerged mid-quarrel.

"I tell you, Albert Wellington is a suspect. I saw him—" Mrs Dunlop broke off abruptly upon noticing Eleanor and Nathaniel. Colour already high in her round face deepened. "I—err—umm, hello there. We were just... well... umm."

Mr Dunlop, as lean as his wife was plump, gave a stiff nod, his ill-fitting wig shifting precariously to the right. "What my darling wife means to say is that we are off to the kitchen in search of a good cup of tea. Care to join us?"

Mrs Dunlop shot him a scowl, making it plain which of the two regarded the game with greater seriousness.

"Thank you, but we are just stretching our legs before the evening's entertainment." Nathaniel began to steer Eleanor past them.

"Wait!" Mrs Dunlop leaned forward conspiratorially. "Would you be willing to trade suspects or clues? It seems most people are forming small alliances."

"We have uncovered no suspects as yet," Nathaniel said.

Mrs Dunlop sighed in disappointment.

Eleanor, taking pity on the woman, glanced back over her shoulder. "You might find it profitable to speak with Leo Vaunt."

At once, Mrs Dunlop brightened. "Oh, thank you! We shall seek him out at once."

As they walked away, Mr Dunlop's voice drifted after them. "We are going to the kitchens first, and that is the end of it."

When they were out of earshot, Nathaniel looked down at Eleanor with an amused glint in his eye. "What possessed you to provide them with a suspect?"

"I thought it only fair, since she unwittingly confirmed Albert Wellington to us."

"Not intentionally."

"No, but still…"

"You are too soft-hearted. I thought you wished to win this game."

"I do," Eleanor insisted, though in truth, her thoughts had wandered elsewhere. Could she, in good conscience, accept a week's holiday from a woman she planned to betray? Or even report the Christmas Bauble's whereabouts to the authorities? A deep breath did little to steady her resolve. She had been engaged for a purpose, and yet, at that moment, she recognised with startling clarity that she would do nothing to bring distress upon the delightful Mrs Winterbourne. She determined right then to return her fee to Mr Fenwick.

"Are you unwell?"

Eleanor turned to Nathaniel, a smile forming. "On the contrary—I am enjoying myself. And you, sir, are an excellent partner in crime."

Their course led them through the wide corridors, past ancestral portraits whose painted eyes seemed to follow their progress. A sharp winter light spilled through the tall windows, casting angular shadows across the chequered floor. The house was quieter now, the murmur of distant conversation subdued, as though Winterbourne Hall itself conspired to keep its secrets.

At last, they reached the conservatory, where golden afternoon light poured through the tall glass panes, illuminating the delicate ferns and citrus trees housed within. A faint scent of earth and orange blossom lingered in the air, lending the space an unnatural warmth for the season. Mrs Sophia De'Luciosi sat amidst this greenery, seated upon a cushioned bench.

She had exchanged the grandeur of her earlier attire for a more comfortable wrap of plum-coloured silk, though she retained a certain ostentation in the heavy rings adorning her fingers. She lifted her gaze as they approached, her expression one of mild curiosity, as if untroubled by the day's earlier dramatics.

"My dears," she greeted them, folding her hands in her lap. "I suppose you have come to interrogate me. How utterly thrilling."

Nathaniel inclined his head. "That would depend on your answers."

Eleanor took a seat opposite her, regarding the woman with measured scrutiny. "You knew Lady Genevieve." It was not a question.

Sophia gave a delicate sigh. "We had an acquaintance, yes. A woman of great... presence, would you not agree?"

"Presence can be interpreted in many ways," Nathaniel said.

"Indeed," Sophia replied. "She was not a woman easily ignored."

"And yet, someone wished to silence her forever," Eleanor said. "Do you know why?"

Sophia trailed her fingers over the armrest of her chair in idle thought. "Oh, my dear, Lady Genevieve was rather too fond of entanglements. She had a way of collecting people—drawing them in, making them feel indispensable, only to discard them when they stopped amusing her. I should imagine more than one person wished her ill, though who among them possessed the inclination for murder, I cannot say."

Nathaniel exchanged a glance with Eleanor. "And did you notice anything unusual since arriving at Winterbourne Hall?"

For a moment, Sophia hesitated. Then, with a languid stretch, she leaned forward, voice lowering as though imparting some delicious piece of gossip. "I did see her arguing with Albert Wellington not ten minutes after we arrived."

"Arguing?" Eleanor inquired.

"Oh, quite so," Sophia assured them. "And with no small degree of fervour. I daresay there was something between them—once, at least. He appeared to be pleading his case, but she…" She hesitated, a flicker of amusement in her expression. "Let us say her manner was less than yielding. I caught only fragments, yet sufficient to discern that whatever understanding once existed between them had been severed. And not, I think, by his hand."

Eleanor regarded her thoughtfully. "You are certain?"

Sophia's eyes shone with quiet satisfaction. "My dear, I never mistake the nature of a quarrel where affairs of the heart are concerned."

A pause settled between them, broken only by the faint rustling of leaves in the warm conservatory air. Eleanor turned the revelation over in her mind, weighing its significance. A scorned lover, a dispute overheard—Albert Wellington had, in an instant, become a figure of great interest.

"That is… most illuminating," Nathaniel said. "And does Albert know that you overheard?"

Sophia's smile was deliberate, edged with mischief. "If he does not, he shall soon enough."

Eleanor exchanged a glance with Nathaniel. Their inquiry had taken yet another turn. Rising from her seat, she paused. "Sophia, may I ask—have you any notion why someone would place a drop of blood on your spoon? It seems a most singular thing to do."

Sophia's colour faded, her expression growing uncharacteristically solemn. "I have heard that to receive such a mark is to receive a warning."

"A warning?" Nathaniel frowned. "And why should anyone wish to warn you? Do you believe it was the murderer?"

Sophia shook her head. "To both your questions, I have not the faintest idea."

*****

The makeshift constabulary had established their domain in the drawing room, where the guests were summoned one by one to endure an examination most exacting. Heavy damask curtains muffled the speculations of those awaiting their turn, while a grand clock on the mantel chimed the quarter-hour with unwavering solemnity.

Eleanor and Nathaniel were led forth together, their expressions schooled into careful civility befitting the occasion, yet hiding their enjoyment of the game that brimmed beneath the surface and lent sparkles to their eyes.

The elder of the two officers, a grizzled man with an imperious brow and a presence that suggested he spent much of his life uncovering the misdeeds of lesser men, regarded them from behind a pair of steel-rimmed spectacles.

His junior, a fresh-faced fellow who bore his uniform with an air of determined officiousness, fixed them with a look he perhaps intended to be piercing.

"You will, of course, understand, madam, sir, that in an inquiry of this nature, no person is above suspicion," the elder intoned. "It would be of great assistance if you were to recount your movements on the evening in question."

Eleanor gave a solemn nod. "I fear I can offer nothing of particular note. The evening proceeded much as one might expect. There was music, conversation, a most diverting supper, and then—" she hesitated, allowing just the right measure of solemnity to darken her tone, "—the unfortunate discovery."

Nathaniel stood at Eleanor's side with his customary ease. "Miss Carstone and I were in one another's company in the moments preceding the event. Having only just been introduced, we were engaged in polite conversation. At no time did either of us leave the ballroom."

The younger officer made a noise of acknowledgement, retrieving a small leather-bound notebook from his pocket. "And you observed nothing untoward? No sign of sudden illness? No change in Lady Genevieve's manner?"

Eleanor exchanged a glance with Nathaniel before replying, "Nothing beyond the ordinary trifles one might expect at such a gathering. We were strangers to her, you understand, and cannot say whether her behaviour differed from her usual self."

The young officer scribbled in his notebook, nodding as he did so. "Yes, yes… in light of the arsenic—" He stopped, his hand stilling.

The room, which had been filled with the quiet scratch of his pen, became silent. Eleanor caught the faintest flicker of surprise in Nathaniel's expression, though he masked it well.

The elder officer turned, slow and deliberate, his gaze fixing on his subordinate with the squint of a man accustomed to dealing with youthful indiscretion. "Arsenic. A most singular word, and one which, I believe, has not yet been introduced to this company."

The young officer paled. "I — that is—"

"Loose lips sink ships, young man," his superior interrupted, his tone now edged with quiet authority, "and win one a date at Newgate Prison and even the gallows."

Enjoying the theatrics of the actors, Eleanor kept her gaze steady, though her mind raced. Arsenic—administered before the fatal blow?

Falling into his role with ease, Nathaniel clasped his hands behind his back. "How enlightening. One wonders, then, if the matter is graver than we first supposed—if such a thing should be possible. Maybe more than one person had it in for the delightful lady?"

The elder officer snorted. "It would be well if you wondered less, sir, and spoke only when required."

Eleanor suppressed a laugh. A dangerous 'game' was afoot, and the clues were multiplying!

*****

Eleanor and Nathaniel withdrew from the drawing room, the revelation of the arsenic giving them something to think about. The grumblings of the actors faded as they stepped into the corridor.

"We must find Albert Wellington," Nathaniel said. "If Sophia is to be believed, he had cause to resent Lady Genevieve, and I should like to hear his account before the police twist it into something more sinister."

Eleanor nodded. "Indeed. And if he is as heartbroken as Sophia hinted, it may not take much persuasion to have him confess the depth of his feelings."

A brief inquiry with a passing footman led them to the library where they found Albert Wellington seated in a high-backed chair amid the scent of leather-bound volumes and the faint crackle of a dying fire. His dark, wavy hair was dishevelled, as though he had run his hands through it one too many times.

There was a carelessness to his appearance—that suggested a man troubled by thought or drink. His eyes, a deep chestnut brown, flicked toward them as they entered, wary yet resigned.

"If you've come to accuse me, I would rather we dispense with the pretence," he said, setting aside the tumbler of brandy in his hand. "I imagine half the house suspects me already."

Eleanor took a seat opposite him, opening her notebook. "Then you will not mind answering a few questions."

A humourless smile ghosted across Albert's lips. "Ask what you will."

Nathaniel remained standing, studying the man before him. "It has come to our attention that you and Lady Genevieve had something of a disagreement on your arrival at the Hall."

Albert's fingers tightened around the armrest of his chair. He was silent for a moment, then gave a small nod. "That much is true."

"Would you care to elaborate?" Eleanor prompted.

Albert let out a slow breath. "I was in love with her." He gave a short, bitter laugh. "Or, at the very least, I believed myself to be. She was unlike any woman I had ever known—charming, sharp-witted, ungovernable. I thought I understood her, but it seems I was mistaken. The night before the gathering, she told me she was quite bored with me and wished to move on."

Eleanor studied his face, searching for deception, but found only pain. "And had she found another?"

Albert shook his head. "She did not say. Only that she desired something... new. It was not the first time she had cast someone aside, but I had been foolish enough to think I might be different."

Nathaniel's voice was steady. "Did you kill her, Albert?"

Albert met his gaze unflinchingly. "No."

The word was simple, unembellished. If the clue was to be believed, he had spoken the truth.

The tension in Eleanor's shoulders eased, though only a bit. She fought off the urge to scribble out his name in her notebook. "Then someone else wished to see her dead. And I should like to know who and why."

They stepped out of the library with haste. The heavy door clicked shut behind them, leaving Albert Wellington to his thoughts, brandy, and well-acted melancholy.

A sharp glance in Nathaniel's direction betrayed her displeasure. "You might have consulted me before asking him outright. You are only permitted one such question, and now you have wasted ours."

Nathaniel tugged at his jumper as if straightening it, his expression unreadable. "I saw an opportunity and took it. I think jealousy the number one motive for murder. Would you rather we had danced around the matter and risked ambiguity?"

Eleanor halted in the corridor, turning to face him. "I would rather we had exercised caution."

His lips twitched, as if he found her scolding amusing. "Then we shall be more judicious next time."

Eleanor mastered her irritation. It would do no good to quarrel further. The afternoon had been long, and her patience wore thin.

"I'm going to rest for a while, I think best when well-rested."

Nathaniel inclined his head, a knowing glint in his eyes. "Then I bid you good afternoon, Miss Carstone. May you be well rested before this evening's entertainment begins. We are running out of time."

Eleanor did not dignify that with a response. She swept past him and made her way upstairs.

Chapter 5

NATHANIEL BLACKWOOD SAT at the walnut writing desk in his room, his fingers hovering over the laptop keyboard as he considered his next sentence. The glow of the screen illuminated his face, casting sharp lines across his features. He had written more than he had intended—notes that danced between curiosity and admiration, between delight and bewilderment. With a sigh, he scrolled up to review his work.

To step over the threshold of Winterbourne Hall is to leave behind the twenty-first century and find oneself quite inexplicably transported to the world of Miss Austen's creation. The effect is not limited to mere costume, nor is it confined to the absurdly faithful architecture of the house itself.

No, the true marvel of Winterbourne is its people. From butler to chambermaid, from footman to cook, all conduct themselves with a devotion to their roles that might well astonish even the most ardent historical re-enactor. It is not simply that they wear the clothes of another age; they wear its manners, its customs, its very speech. There is no modern slang to be overheard, no idle check of a phone, no flicker of the twenty-first century in their gazes.

One might address a footman with a perfectly reasonable query—'Do you happen to know if there is Wi-Fi?'—only to be met with a bow and an utterly earnest, 'I do not, sir, but I shall inquire with Mrs Winterbourne, if you wish it.' It is, in short, a theatre without an audience, a play in which all are both performer and spectator, and

one can only wonder whether they have, in some
curious fashion, become the roles they have
assumed.

Nathaniel leaned back in his chair, pressing his fingers against his temple. It was, if nothing else, a fascinating study in eccentricity, and yet he found his mind straying from Mrs Winterbourne's whims and her devoted household. Instead, it wandered to Eleanor Carstone.

He had not expected her.

For four years, the idea of love, of even the smallest flicker of interest, had been as distant to him as the stars. He had buried that part of himself along with his wife, and he had been content—so he had thought—to leave it there.

But Eleanor…

The delicate upturn of her nose, the curve of her soft pink lips—something about her stirred a longing he hadn't believed himself capable of feeling again.

Those deep brown eyes, intelligent and keen, as if they saw beyond the surface of things had looked at him as no one had in years. He could not say that he believed in love at first sight, for that was the stuff of fiction, of fairy tales—of Austen novels. But love at second sight? At third? He was beginning to suspect he might be a fool enough man to believe in that.

A part of him recoiled at his deception. He had not intended to lie. An author, he had told her. But was he not writing? Was he not filling pages with words, even if those words were destined for a column rather than a novel?

His assignment for *The Society Review*, a magazine read by the country's elite, had brought him here under the pretence of curiosity—an exposé on the peculiar, endlessly charming Mrs Winterbourne and her living, breathing Regency world.

And yet, somewhere between note-taking and observation, between playing his role and watching Eleanor play hers, the lines had begun to blur. No, he would tell her the truth before they left Winterbourne. He owed her that.

Exhaling, Nathaniel shut the laptop and stood, stretching out the tension in his shoulders. There would be time enough for confessions later. For now, there was an evening's entertainment to prepare for—and Eleanor would be there, stepping through candlelit corridors, her laughter echoing through the halls, tempting him further into something he had not thought himself ready for.

And yet, here he was.

*****

Eleanor sat at the small, elegant writing desk in her room, the glow of her laptop screen illuminating her delicate features. She had just finished composing her email, her fingers lingering over the keys as she reread her message.

From: Miss Carstone
Dear Mr Fenwick,
After studying the Christmas decoration at length, it is my professional opinion that this ball is indeed part of the Prince Albert collection. I attach a full breakdown of my analysis along with several photographs for your appraisal.
The inscription reads 'Dein auf ewig, Albert'— 'Yours forever, Albert'—which, as you know, differs from your stolen bauble's engraving, 'Für immer in men Herzen.'
Please let me know if I can be of further assistance.

With a deep breath, she hit send.

The response came almost immediately.

> *Ms Carstone, thank you for your swift work. This is indeed useful information. However, I have just received troubling news—Baron and Baroness von Elsner have also had their Prince Albert Christmas Bauble stolen just two weeks ago. Of the five known baubles, three are now confirmed missing. Please advise Mrs Winterbourne to keep hers well protected. I fear there may be a pattern here.*

Eleanor's stomach tightened. Three of the five baubles— gone. And now only Mrs Winterbourne's and one other remained. The likelihood of it being a coincidence was slim. Could it be a series of unrelated thefts, or was someone systematically targeting these priceless ornaments?

Closing the laptop, she sighed and reached for her notebook.

Turning the pages, she found the list of suspects in the murder mystery game, frowning, she studied the names.

1 — Ms Angela Pellidoc, reason still unclear

2 — Sally Monterey, possible reason revenge

3 — Leo Vaunt – possible blackmail motive

4 — Albert Wellington, reason, jealousy (she put a thick line through his name; he was no longer a viable suspect)

5 — Mrs Sophia De'Luciosi, the Italian beauty could have several reasons, including jealousy and revenge

6 — Who?

The sixth suspect remained a mystery. Who was playing the role? How had they managed to stay hidden? She chewed the end of her pencil, her mind racing. If she couldn't identify them, she would have to flush them out. Perhaps a few more strategic alliances with the other guests would help.

The list of names blurred and swam before her eyes, when they settled she focused on Sophia De'Luciosi. Delicious—so obvious, why hadn't she seen it before? Who was left? Wellington, Beef Wellington? A laugh bubbled inside her and spilled over. They are all related to food. One thing became clear, she needed to analyse the guest names again and find the sixth actor.

Right now, she needed to finish getting ready. She checked the clock. Six p.m. Time was slipping away. They had until four the next day to solve the mystery.

Frustrated, Eleanor snapped the notebook shut and stood, crossing the room to her dressing table. In the mirror, her reflection met her gaze—her coffee eyes bright with determination, her lips rose-tinted for the evening ahead.

With delicate twists and loops, she pinned her dark brown hair in an elegant Regency style, leaving a few soft curls to frame her face, giving her a look of effortless grace.

Her gown, a rich shade of cornflower blue, draped over her frame in flowing folds of silk, the empire waistline accentuating her figure. Beneath it, the gentle constraint of her corset kept her posture straight and her waist subtly defined. The puffed sleeves sat just off her shoulders, revealing the graceful slope of her collarbone, her neckline left bare of any adornment. The only jewellery she wore was a pair of delicate drop earrings— fake pearls, but beautiful nonetheless, catching the light as she moved.

She reached for her lace fan, the ivory frame cool against her fingertips, and took a steadying breath. It was just a game. Just an evening of entertainment. So why did she feel as though something more significant was unfolding? And why was the handsome face of one particular guest forever in her mind?

With one last glance at her reflection, she turned and left the room, her skirts rustling as she moved.

*****

The grand hallway was alive with warmth and festivity.

Before the twinkling Christmas tree, a choir of carol singers stood in perfect formation, their red velvet capes trimmed with white fur lending them a festive elegance. Their voices wove together in a harmony so rich that a shiver ran down Eleanor's spine. Around the candle sconces, bundles of fresh cinnamon and nutmeg released their warm, spiced fragrance into the air. The flickering candlelight caught the deep green and gold decorations, making them shimmer as though dusted with magic, casting a soft, golden glow over the gathered guests.

She felt the tension ease from her shoulders as she listened, letting the music wrap around her like a comforting embrace. Now that she was officially on holiday, she felt a carefree and rather merry attitude descend on her.

When the final notes of *God Rest Ye Merry Gentlemen* faded, the carollers dipped their heads in a graceful bow, and the guests erupted into polite applause before making their way into the dining room.

The quartet in the corner struck up a soft, elegant melody as they entered, the polished mahogany table gleaming under the glow of the chandeliers. The silverware sparkled, the crystal glasses catching the light like tiny prisms.

As she hesitated near her seat, Nathaniel appeared at her side.

He had not spoken to her since she had come downstairs, but she had felt his presence, his gaze lingering just long enough to make her breath hitch. Now, he moved beside her, effortlessly sliding her chair back for her.

"May I sit beside you?" His voice was low, smooth, edged with something unreadable.

She glanced up at him, lost in the way the candlelight caught in his dark eyes. "Of course."

As she settled into her chair, his hand brushed her shoulder, sending a ripple of awareness through her. Warmth that had nothing to do with the fire crackling in the hearth unfurled in her chest. Foolish to react that way—like a girl experiencing her first infatuation.

Yet her heart beat a little too fast, her breath a fraction too shallow. The urge to kiss him came swift and unexpected, absurd in its intensity. She reached for her glass, taking a deep sip of Champagne, as if the chilled, effervescent liquid might temper the sudden rush of heated feeling.

She had only met him a few hours ago and didn't know him. For all she knew, he could be married with six children— all devotedly waiting for him at home! Heat flamed in her cheeks at the thought, and she hoped, beyond reason, that wasn't the case.

And yet, when he turned to her with that faint, knowing smile, she found she didn't care nearly as much as she ought to.

*****

The meal unfolded in a blur of conversation and laughter.

As wine and Champagne flowed, the guests grew giddy, their voices rising with each course. Some swapped theories about the game, conspiratorial whispers passing between them. Others cast logic aside, declaring their suspicions with wild enthusiasm.

Eleanor listened, half-engaged, but her mind remained tangled in questions. The stolen baubles. The missing suspect. The lingering warmth of Nathaniel's touch.

Eleanor lifted her Champagne flute to her lips, though she didn't taste the bubbles as she stole another glance at Nathaniel. The candelabra cast a warm glow over his sharp features, the flicker of the flames reflecting in his resplendent eyes as he studied her with quiet amusement. It was unnerving, this way he looked at her—as if he saw far more than she was ready to reveal.

Forcing herself to focus, she cleared her throat. "So, Nathaniel, where do you come from?"

He set down his wine glass, and turned to face her, the movement bringing them just a little closer. "Originally? Oxfordshire. From a village not too dissimilar from this one, though admittedly without a grand house playing host to Regency theatrics. And you?"

"London," she said, swirling the Champagne in her glass.

He smiled. "That makes sense, lots of museums to visit. You seem rather at home surrounded by artefacts and puzzles."

Eleanor laughed softly. "And you? I imagine an author needs a certain environment to work in. Do you live in Oxfordshire still?"

Nathaniel hesitated for half a second before replying, "No, I live in London now."

It was a simple answer, but something about the pause caught her attention. She parted her lips to ask another question, but the words never came. His gaze had settled on her mouth, and for a moment, she forgot what they had been talking about.

The surrounding conversations blurred into background noise. It was astonishing, the pull she felt towards him. As if some invisible thread had tied them together the moment they met, drawing them ever closer despite her best intentions.

And then — "I say," boomed a voice, cutting through the hum of conversation like a cannon shot. "That clue in Lady Genevieve's bedroom was a giveaway. Far too easy, if you ask me."

The moment shattered. Eleanor and Nathaniel both turned to the source of the voice at the same time.

Colonel Montague sat at the far end of the table, one elbow propped on the polished wood, his fingers idly tapping the rim of his port glass. A man of ample build with a ruddy complexion, he bore the look of someone rather too fond of pork pies—his waistcoat struggling to contain the evidence of his indulgences. As he took another sip of port, his thick moustache twitched in satisfaction, clearly pleased with his own deduction.

Nathaniel arched a brow. "I didn't know we had access to her room."

Before Colonel Montague could respond, Mrs Winterbourne interjected with her usual air of calm authority. "Yes, well, now that the police have gone, there are no places of interest that remain off limits. Except, of course, the cornered-off areas."

Her words sent a ripple of interest through the guests, and Eleanor caught the quick glance Nathaniel sent her way. The game had just shifted, and she wondered how quickly they could leave the dining room.

*****

Having most sensibly declined dessert—Eleanor, fearing her corset might stage a violent rebellion should she dare another morsel—had instead proposed a little stroll to aid digestion. Nathaniel, ever the obliging companion, offered to escort her. Thus, with expressions of perfect innocence, they rose from the table and made a slow, deliberate retreat from the dining room.

The moment they were out of sight, however, all pretence of decorum vanished. With a conspiratorial glance, they darted towards the grand staircase, their shoes skimming the plush carpeting as they took the stairs two at a time. Their laughter, suppressed though it was, echoed in the empty hall, making them feel like schoolchildren sneaking away from a chaperone's watchful eye.

Upon reaching the corridor above, they hurried to their goal—the door plainly labelled Lady Genevieve. Pausing only to catch their breath, they exchanged a final glance, their faces alight with mischief, before slipping inside.

The room, a vision of pastel elegance, bore all the expected marks of its fictional occupant. A faint scent of lavender lingered in the air, and a dressing table, adorned with ivory-handled brushes and delicate perfume bottles, stood as a shrine to Lady Genevieve's vanity.

Their search began in earnest, though it was difficult to say which was the greater distraction—the thrilling prospect of discovery or the far more immediate allure of each other. Every brush of a sleeve, every accidental meeting of hands, sent an unmistakable frisson through the air. One moment they were whispering like conspirators, the next stifling their laughter as though the walls themselves might betray them.

"Look at this," Nathaniel said suddenly, waving her over to the dressing table.

Eleanor leaned in, so close that a mere breath separated them. He held up a torn page from The Morning Post, dated 12th June 1880. The faded print detailed a series of daring highway robberies, carried out by a masked figure known only as The Midnight Rider. The article, dripping in melodrama, speculated that the elusive criminal was of noble birth, given his refined manners and eloquent speech.

Eleanor's eyes sparkled as she read. "Didn't Genevieve mention being robbed last night before her unfortunate demise?"

Nathaniel nodded, his lips curving into a wry smile. "It does seem too much of a coincidence to ignore. Though, I confess, I was paying little attention to her words at the time—my mind was otherwise occupied."

Eleanor looked up, only to find his gaze fixed upon her, the meaning behind his words utterly unmistakable. The way he studied her—so intent, so singularly focused—sent warmth flooding through her.

She blushed, wholly against her will, though she could not quite bring herself to look away. "You are incorrigible."

Their moment, heady with unsaid things, was rudely shattered by a sharp intake of breath.

Both spun around.

A chambermaid stood in the doorway, eyes wide with distress. She was perhaps in her mid-thirties, with fair curls peeking from beneath her white linen cap. Her black gown, neatly pressed, bore the crisp apron of her station, though she was presently using a handkerchief to dab at her eyes.

Eleanor stepped forward at once. "Are you quite well? Can we be of any assistance?"

The maid, Elizabeth, gave a watery sniff, wringing her hands in distress. "Oh, miss, I am in terrible trouble! Lady Genevieve's ruby brooch—it's gone! She was wearing it when she dressed for dinner, I know because I helped her get ready. It's worth a fortune, and someone told the police they noticed it missing when they saw her on the library floor. Which means—" Her voice wavered, and she clutched her apron as if it might steady her. "Which means someone took it. And now Mrs Winterbourne says that if it isn't found, I'll be dismissed—without so much as a reference!"

Eleanor exchanged a glance with Nathaniel before turning back to the maid. "That hardly seems fair. Surely Mrs Winterbourne does not believe you had a hand in its disappearance?"

Elizabeth sniffled and nodded. "Aye, miss, but I was the first to find Lady Genevieve. But I didn't touch her, I swear it. I went straight to Mrs Winterbourne. But you know how it is—when something goes missing, they always look to the servants first."

Eleanor straightened, her pretence at indignation growing. "Well, then, we shall just have to prove that you had nothing to do with it. Nathaniel?" She turned to him with a look of expectation.

Nathaniel sighed, though there was a glint of fun in his eyes. "Ah, and here I thought we were merely investigating murder. It seems we are now in pursuit of a jewel thief as well."

Then, his expression grew more thoughtful. "Or perhaps the two are one and the same—what if the murderer took it?"

A hush settled between them as the idea took shape. Eleanor tapped her pencil against her chin before setting to work, scribbling notes as fast as her hand would allow. Had the brooch been stolen in haste, snatched from Lady Genevieve's lifeless form by a panicked killer? A slight of misdirection, perhaps to throw the police of the murderer's scent. Or had it been taken by someone else, an opportune thief who saw their moment and grabbed it?

"That is indeed serious," he said gravely, though there was an unmistakable gleam of intrigue and merriment in his eyes. "And you are sure Lady Genevieve wore it last night, no mistakes?"

Elizabeth nodded fervently. "Aye, sir! I helped pin it on her and a jewel so big is quite unforgettable."

"Then we shall help you search, let us begin in this room on the slim chance that you are mistaken, and that she returned it here herself before the dreadful event took place," Eleanor said at once.

Nathaniel sighed, though it was the sigh of a man who had fully resigned himself to the adventure. "We were meant to be investigating a murder, but what is a little theft along the way?"

Despite their thorough search—pulling back draperies, checking beneath furniture, even upending the embroidered cushions—no brooch was to be found.

Just as they were debating their next course of action, the sound of approaching footsteps reached them. The door swung open, and six other guests spilled into the room, each bearing the expression of an eager detective hot on the trail.

Seeing no further opportunity to continue their private investigation, Eleanor and Nathaniel withdrew, leaving Elizabeth to recount her misfortune to the new arrivals.

As they made their way back down the staircase, Eleanor glanced at Nathaniel. "A nobleman-turned-highwayman, a stolen brooch, a blunt instrument murder—this mystery is growing wilder by the moment."

Nathaniel grinned. "Indeed. And I, for one, am enjoying every second."

*****

Entering the ballroom, Eleanor and Nathaniel found themselves enveloped in the warm glow of candlelight and the lilting strains of violin. The orchestra, tucked into a corner beneath a towering Christmas garland, played a lively country dance, and the polished floor gleamed beneath the swirl of silks, satins, and embroidered waistcoats. The guests had outdone themselves—here, a gentleman in full military regalia, there, a lady with pearls woven into her hair, the very image of an Austen heroines.

Mrs Winterbourne, of course, was the most resplendent of all. The petite yet commanding woman was in her element, fluttering a lace-trimmed fan as she held court amongst admirers. Her gown was a marvel—deep emerald green, with gold embroidery twining over the bodice like ivy and sleeves that billowed with dramatic effect. Her silver-grey hair was swept into an elaborate chignon, adorned with a delicate tiara that winked as she stood beneath a chandelier. Her stormy eyes sparkled with mischief as she waved off another offer to dance.

"Oh no, my dear sir," she trilled to a persistent gentleman. "My affections are soundly engaged—with the art of observation. Besides, a woman must ration her exertions lest she become utterly undone before the night is through."

Eleanor and Nathaniel exchanged an amused glance, standing close—so close that when Nathaniel shifted his weight, his arm brushed against hers.

"Are we to take a break from our sleuthing, then?" He offered her a glass of champagne.

"For a little while," Eleanor conceded, taking a sip. "It would be a shame not to enjoy all of this. Consider the effort everyone puts in."

"Indeed," Nathaniel said, though he was not looking at the guests.

Eleanor glanced up and found his eyes fixed on her. Her breath hitched. The air between them charged, an unspoken understanding humming in the space where their fingers nearly touched.

Chapter 6

NATHANIEL CLEARED HIS THROAT and extended a hand. "Would you do me the honour of a dance?"

Eleanor arched a brow. "I regret to inform you that I am quite without a dance card."

"Scandalous!" His eyes twinkled. "But I suppose I shall have to take my chances."

She placed her hand in his, and they moved onto the floor. The moment his palm settled on the small of her back, a delicious shiver ran through her. His touch was warm, steady, protective. How long had it been since she had danced like this, since she had felt the thrill of anticipation from something as simple as a hand at her waist?

Nathaniel held her gaze as they moved in time with the music, his grip firm yet careful, as though he were committing every detail of the moment to memory.

"You dance well," she said, a little breathless.

"I have an excellent partner," he returned, voice low, a tad husky.

Eleanor had the absurd urge to press closer, to let go of everything else but this—this crackling, undeniable pull between them.

When the dance ended, they hesitated, standing too close, neither willing to break the spell. Eleanor knew, with a certainty that unsettled her, that she did not wish to return to the reality of the party—not yet.

Nathaniel must have sensed it too. He took her hand, fingers warm against hers. "Come with me."

Without hesitation, she followed him out of the ballroom, down the quiet corridor, and into the library.

The room was dimly lit, the fire in the grate reduced to a flickering glow. Floor-to-ceiling bookshelves cast long shadows, and the scent of old parchment and polished wood wrapped around them like a secret.

Nathaniel turned to face her, his eyes dark, unreadable. The moment stretched, heavy with expectation.

Then he reached for her, his fingers threading into her hair, his touch reverent as though he feared the moment would shatter if he moved too quickly. And then—his lips met hers.

Eleanor scarcely had time to register the softness of his mouth, the way he exhaled as though he had been holding his breath for hours, before the distant sound of approaching footsteps sent them both into action.

Nathaniel tugged her toward the towering velvet curtains, and they slipped behind them just as the library door opened.

Two voices, hushed but brimming with excitement, filled the space.

"Oh, Charlotte," the voice unmistakably belonged to Miss Emma Leighton. "We might know that Leo Vaunt is not the killer now that we have asked him outright, but did you hear what he said about the crime scene?"

Charlotte, shushed her with a warning finger and whispered, "You mean about the window?"

"Yes! A slight breeze coming through, when it should have been locked! That means the murderer could have escaped that way."

A pause, then the rustle of skirts. "What shall we do now?" Emma asked.

"We must find Sophia. Sally hinted this morning that she saw Sophia go to the stables, and you know she doesn't ride. We have to find out why she was there."

Their voices faded as they slipped out of the library, their footsteps hurrying down the corridor.

Eleanor released a breath of laughter, pressing a hand to her lips. "I thought I would giggle and give us away."

Nathaniel grinned, his fingers still lightly clasping hers. "Good thing you didn't—because now you have another name to strike off the list." He leaned in, his breath warm against her ear. "Leo Vaunt. Two down, four to go."

Eleanor shook her head puzzled. "Yes—but who is the sixth actor?"

They exchanged a knowing look, and both of them shrugged.

"When we have time, we need to go through the list of names again and search out another name linked to food. I have skipped over them a couple of times but I don't think I am paying enough attention."

Nathaniel agreed. "We should do that… in the morning."

*****

The moment they stepped back into the ballroom, Eleanor and Nathaniel exchanged a look of silent understanding.

"We should split up," Nathaniel said. "I'll see what else I can learn from Ms Pellidoc. You take Sophia."

Eleanor nodded. "Meet me back here in twenty minutes?"

His chin set in determination, "Unless I find myself in over my head."

"Then I shall have to rescue you," she said, before slipping away into the crowd.

Eleanor soon spotted Sophia lingering near the refreshment table, a glass of cordial in hand. The slim woman was dressed in a high-waisted gown of pale lavender, her fair curls pinned back with delicate silver combs. She looked up as Eleanor approached, a flicker of wariness in her eyes.

"Miss De'Luciosi," Eleanor greeted with an easy smile. "I wonder if I might trouble you for a word?"

Sophia hesitated before nodding. "Of course."

Eleanor glanced at the dance floor, where Charlotte and Emma Leighton had been waylaid by two enthusiastic gentlemen asking for a set. The sisters, side-tracked in their murder investigation, exchanged glances of annoyance at spotting Eleanor with Sophia before laughing and allowing themselves to be swept into the dance.

"Tell me," Eleanor began, lowering her voice, "why were you seen going to the stables this morning?"

Sophia blinked. "Oh! Well, I—" She glanced about, as if to ensure no one was eavesdropping. "I went for a walk before breakfast and thought I heard something unusual from inside. I peered in but saw nothing—just an empty stable, a few dusty tools. I didn't think much of it, so I left."

"But you do not ride?" Eleanor pressed.

Sophia flushed. "No, I do not."

"Then why go that way at all?"

The woman hesitated. "I... well, I suppose I was just curious. It felt odd, that's all."

Eleanor considered this. "Why is that?"

"I couldn't shake the sensation. It was as if... well, you know when the hairs on the back of your neck stand up? Like that. I am sure someone followed me." She gave a small, embarrassed laugh. "But then again, I had spent the *entire* night before locked in conversation with Colonel Montague. He's rather a bore, you see, and after an hour of discussing military strategy, one begins to imagine things."

Eleanor relaxed, her mind slotting this information into place. "The entire evening, you say?"

Sophia sighed. "Oh, indeed. I couldn't escape him. He told me all about his theories on modern warfare—apparently, bayonets are an underappreciated art form—and just when I thought he had finished, he went on to lament the sorry state of old country estates."

Eleanor curled her toes in her shoes; if she understood correctly, Sophia had just unveiled her alibi. "What do you mean?"

"He said it was a pity there were no horses at Winterbourne anymore. He hoped Mrs Winterbourne wouldn't turn the stables into one of those fashionable cafés like so many grand houses do these days. He was quite impassioned on the subject."

Eleanor smiled. "You endured quite the ordeal."

"You have no idea," Sophia chuckled fluttering her fan. Then she straightened, as if recalling something. "I've just remembered—he told me he saw someone at the stables yesterday afternoon. That might have prompted my interest in it."

Eleanor's breath caught. "Who?"

"Well, he didn't get a clear look, but from his description—the colour of her gown, her stature—I can only think he meant Lady Genevieve. He said she was talking with someone, but he couldn't see who. Whoever it was stood in the shadows."

Eleanor's mind whirred. "You're certain about this?"

Sophia nodded. "If you don't believe me, you can ask him yourself. But I promise you, he was most put out that he hadn't been able to see more."

Eleanor smiled. "I think you've just given me something useful." Eleanor thanked her and excused herself, her thoughts raced. Maybe something had been hidden in the stables, perhaps it was still there.

*****

Meanwhile, across the ballroom, Nathaniel found Angela Pellidoc lounging near a group of gentlemen, holding court as they hung on her every word. She was dressed in an elegant black gown, her dark hair swept into an intricate knot at the nape of her neck. As Nathaniel approached, she met his gaze with an amused smile.

"Mr Blackwood," she purred. "Back for more?"

"Always." He stepped closer. "You strike me as someone who enjoys being in the know."

She chuckled behind her fan. "A woman must have her amusements."

As if on cue, a low laugh came from behind them.

Nathaniel turned to see a gentleman step smoothly into their conversation, a glass of brandy in one hand and a knowing smile on his lips. Of medium height, with a trim figure he carried himself with a self-assured air, his cravat tied in a particularly elaborate fashion that suggested either great vanity or great distaste at the vanity of others.

"My dear, Angela, you wound us," he said in mock despair. "Reducing us all to mere diversions for your fun. What will become of our poor, fragile hearts?"

Angela turned to him with a languid smile. "Mr Rutherford, you and your fragile hearts will recover, I'm sure." She gestured toward a few other gentlemen who had gathered around her, all with the air of men who had found themselves happily ensnared in Angela's web. "These fine gentlemen have been trying to persuade me into a game of cards in the drawing room. Mr Blackwood, do you play?"

Nathaniel, who had been watching this exchange with interest, gave a slight shrug. "On occasion."

Another man stepped forward then, and he was not like the others.

Tall and lean, with dark hair and inky blue eyes, Lord Whitmore had the look of a man who saw more than he let on. His posture relaxed, his smile easy, yet a sharpness pierced his gaze as it flicked over Nathaniel, assessing, measuring.

"Ah, but I fear I already have far too much competition," Lord Whitmore said, taking Angela's hand in his own and pressing a slow, deliberate kiss to her gloved fingers. "And I suspect Mr Blackwood is far too busy sleuthing to indulge in a friendly game." His eyes flickered with amusement as he looked at Nathaniel. "Or am I mistaken?"

Nathaniel's lips curved in a subtle smile. "That depends. Are the stakes worth my time?"

Angela let out a low, throaty laugh. "Oh, I do like you, Mr Blackwood." She withdrew her hand from Whitmore's grasp with a teasing smile. "But I think I'll let you and Lord Whitmore determine which of you is the greater gambler. I, for one, have no intention of losing my pearls over a poor hand."

Lord Whitmore gave a solemn nod. "A wise woman, indeed." Then, turning back to Nathaniel, he added with an almost imperceptible smirk, "Perhaps another time, then. When you are not so… occupied."

"And what about yourself, sir? Do you not participate in the game afoot—or have you already determined the killer's identity?" Nathaniel asked.

Whitmore gave a lazy shrug. "Games are for children, are they not?" Then, turning to Angela, he added, "Now, if the prize were your devoted attention… well, that would be another matter indeed. The murderer would be named, the mystery solved, and the game concluded within the hour."

Angela laughed, the rich sound of a woman well-accustomed to flattery. She tapped his arm with her fan. "Do behave, Lord Whitmore, or I shall be forced to write a letter to your dear wife."

Nathaniel regarded the exchange, his fingers tightening at his side. There was something about Lord Whitmore that unsettled him, though he could not yet say why. It wasn't suspicion—but the man's effortless arrogance, his casual charm, grated on him more than it should have. Who comes to a murder mystery weekend and not take part?

Angela, sensing the moment had run its course, fluttered her fan. "Come along, gentlemen. Let's leave poor Mr Blackwood to his sleuthing before he decides to interrogate us all."

With that, she turned on her heel, her admirers falling into step around her as they made their way to the drawing room. Lord Whitmore lingered a moment, giving Nathaniel a slow, appraising glance before following after them.

Nathaniel found himself gritting his teeth. He hadn't even asked Angela one question. He turned to take in the room and to search out Eleanor.

Having already spotted him, his delightful new acquaintance headed straight for him.

As soon as they were alone, she asked, "How did you get on?"

"As badly as bad can be, I'm afraid. You?"

"I've been able to cross another name off the list."

"Really? Who?"

Eleanor glanced around to ensure no one was in earshot. "Sophia De'Luciosi! The stunning Italian spent all last evening up until the murder pinned down in conversation by Colonel Montague."

"Poor woman!"

They both grinned. "Did you find out nothing at all?" asked Eleanor.

"If you're trying to rub my nose in it, you're doing a good job!"

Eleanor laughed. "Well, I have another snippet of news."

"And pray tell, what is that?"

"I've discovered…"

"Mr Blackwood." Startled, the two turned around to see Angela sweeping back towards them. "Mr Blackwood, I seem to have lost my handkerchief, I wondered…"

Glancing down, Nathaniel saw it on the floor next to his feet. In a swift swoop, he reached down and picked it up. He shook it as if to shake off any dust and then handed it to her.

She winked. "My hero."

Eleanor's cheeks went tomato red.

Nathaniel gave a wry smile. "I suspect Lord Whitmore is going to be awaiting your return with utmost eagerness, Mrs De'Luciosi."

"Indeed he may, but I believe you wanted to ask me a private question?"

"I did, and I will be blunt. I suspect you know far more about Lady Genevieve than you originally let on."

Angela arched a brow. "Do I?"

Nathaniel leaned forward. "She went to the stables when she arrived yesterday afternoon. That is an odd place for a lady to spend her first moments at Winterbourne Hall, don't you think?"

Angela's lips pursed in thought. "It is. And yet, if I were you, I would be less concerned about where Genevieve went and more about what—or who—she expected to find there."

Nathaniel's gaze sharpened. "You mean someone was waiting for her?"

Angela swirled the wine in her glass. "Now, I didn't say that."

Nathaniel sighed. "You do like to be cryptic."

She smiled. "It keeps me young."

As she strode away, Eleanor leaned into Nathaniel. "Sophia just confirmed to me the same thing—Lady Genevieve met with someone at the stables yesterday afternoon." She turned and looked up at him. "I think our next stop has to be the stables."

"Shouldn't we wait until tomorrow when it is light?"

"No. I'm determined to win this game," she chuckled. "Come with me?"

"Well, I'm not letting you go on your own."

They headed into the lobby. On the reception counter, three large torches had been left in plain sight. Nathaniel picked one up. "They're expecting us to go outside."

Stepping through the door, Eleanor glanced at the flickering lanterns illuminating the grounds. The path from Winterbourne Hall to the stables was a treacherous stretch of old, uneven cobbles, glistening from the evening's damp air. Though she had chosen flat-soled slippers for authenticity's sake, she still felt her footing waver as she took the first few steps.

Nathaniel, ever observant, offered his arm again. "May I?"

Eleanor hesitated only a moment before slipping her hand into the crook of his elbow. The warmth of him was steadying, reassuring. She tried not to notice the way her pulse jumped at the simple touch.

Together, they made their way through the night, the soft hush of the wind and distant rustling of trees the only sounds accompanying them.

The old stable loomed ahead, its weathered beams casting long shadows in the moonlight. The scent of hay and aged wood filled the air as they stepped inside, their torch casting golden pools of light against the stalls.

They searched in silence, moving past empty stalls and worn tack.

Eleanor spotted it first—a loose brick in the wall, its edges marked by faint scratches where the cement had been pried away. "Nathaniel," she hissed with excitement.

He was at her side in an instant. Together, they worked the brick free, revealing a small velvet pouch stuffed into the hollow. Eleanor's breath caught as she reached inside, fingers brushing against something cool and hard.

The ruby brooch.

But that was not all. Tucked within the pouch, lay something even more damning—a folded black silk mask, of the kind worn by highwaymen.

Nathaniel grinned and held it up. "Well, this is interesting."

Eleanor's fingers tightened around the brooch. The implications were undeniable.

The murderer hadn't only stolen from Lady Genevieve in the past and the present. He—or she—had killed Genevieve to protect their secret identity.

They exchanged a glance, the discovery bringing them a shared exhilaration.

"The question now," Eleanor said, "is who among the guests is our Midnight Rider?"

Nathaniel nodded. "And why did they hide this here?"

A shiver ran down Eleanor's spine, though she could not say if it was from the cold night air or the knowledge that they were closer than ever to uncovering the truth.

Noticing her shiver, Nathaniel shrugged off his dinner jacket and draped it over her shoulders. "You're frozen."

She pulled it tighter around herself, the lingering warmth of his body heat oddly comforting. "I suppose standing about in dark, drafty stables will do that to a person."

"Then we should go back inside before you turn to ice." They put the clues back in the pouch and replaced it in the hole for the next guest to find. Nathaniel wrapped his arm around her should shoulder and led her out of the stables.

As they made their way toward the house, Eleanor glanced up at him. "I hear the kitchen is always open—do you think they'll make us some hot chocolate?"

Nathaniel chuckled. "I would wager they will if you ask nicely."

True to rumour, the kitchen was still bustling, though most of the staff had retired for the evening. The chubby, rosy-cheeked cook, Mrs Florence Colepepper, sat reading by the roaring fire, dressed in the traditional garb of her station. She looked up as they entered, setting aside her book with an indulgent smile.

"Well now, you looked chilled. What can I do for you?"

Eleanor clasped her hands together in mock supplication. "Would it be terribly improper to beg for a hot chocolate?"

Florence let out a hearty chuckle. "Terribly improper, I might say—but lucky for you, I've a soft spot for guests with good manners. Off with you to the library, and I'll bring your drinks in shortly."

With grateful thanks, they left the warmth of the kitchen and made their way to the library. Once inside, Eleanor settled at a writing desk, pulling out her notebook. She struck a firm line through Sophia De'Luciosi's name, leaving only three suspects remaining. Then, on the sixth mark where she had previously placed a question mark, she wrote one word: highwayman.

Nathaniel, watching over her shoulder, let out a thoughtful hum. "It does have a rather dramatic flair, doesn't it?"

Before Eleanor could reply, the door opened, and the cook bustled in, carrying a tray with two steaming mugs of hot chocolate and a plate of ginger biscuits.

"There now," she said, setting them down with a satisfied nod. "Best way to warm up on a chilly night."

Eleanor wrapped her hands around the mug, inhaling the rich, spiced aroma. She smiled at Nathaniel over the rim. "To solving mysteries."

His lips quirked, "And to staying warm while doing so."

*****

When Eleanor and Nathaniel emerged from the library, the strains of a waltz still drifted through the air, soft and soothing, though the ballroom was now half-empty. Many of the guests had already retired, some exchanging their goodnights as they ascended the grand staircase, others slipping away into waiting taxis, their laughter lingering in the night air.

Nathaniel bent his head, his voice a low murmur, intimate and inviting. "I should like one last dance before the evening ends. Would you grant me the honour?"

He extended his hand, and without hesitation, she placed hers in it. His fingers closed around hers and the faintest of tremors rushed through her.

Together, they strolled into the ballroom, and as though they had planned it, moved at once into a gentle waltz, seamlessly falling into step as the last notes of Johann Strauss's *The Emperor Waltz* floated through the candlelit room.

Their eyes met, and in that instant, the world beyond them ceased to exist. There was no game, no murder, no hidden mysteries—only the quiet intimacy of the moment, the unspoken understanding that something had begun between them, something neither could deny.

Nathaniel reached up, his touch feather-light, and brushed a stray curl from her cheek. Warmth, both thrilling and unfamiliar, spread through her, setting her senses alight. Never before had she been so aware of the space between her and another, nor of how desperately she wished for it to disappear altogether.

And then, too soon, the music ceased. One of the musicians, an elderly gentleman with kind eyes and a formal manner, set down his violin and offered a small bow. "I do hope you enjoyed the music this evening, ladies and gentlemen."

There was a smattering of applause from the few remaining guests. Eleanor and Nathaniel stepped apart, though his fingers lingered just a moment longer upon hers before he released her. The hush that followed seemed to hum with unspoken words.

Silently, he offered his arm once more, and together they ascended the stairs, neither speaking, as though to do so would shatter the delicate spell that bound them. At her chamber door, she turned to him, her pulse fluttering like a caged bird.

Nathaniel raised his hands, cupping her face with a tenderness that stole the breath from her lungs. Slowly— exquisitely so—he leaned in, his lips brushing hers with a care that made the moment all the more intoxicating. The world tilted, faded, disappeared, until there was nothing but the warmth of his mouth, the evocative musky scent of him, the steady press of his hands against her skin.

When at last he drew away, his gaze remained fixed on hers, dark and unreadable, though his voice, when he spoke, was impossibly soft. "Goodnight, my beautiful sleuthing partner. Until the morrow."

With one last lingering touch, he stepped back, and Eleanor, unable to trust her voice, slipped inside and closed the door.

For a moment, she remained there, her back pressed against the wood, her fingers rising of their own accord to touch her lips, as though to convince herself the moment had truly happened. A slow, helpless smile curved her mouth.

"I think I'm falling in love with you, Mr Blackwood."

Chapter 7

ELEANOR ENTERED THE breakfast room to find Nathaniel already seated at a table by the bay windows, a cup of coffee in hand and an open newspaper beside his plate. He glanced up as she approached, a knowing glint in his eyes, but if he expected her to speak of last night, he would be disappointed. She offered a composed smile and took the seat opposite him.

"Morning," she said, reaching for her napkin.

"Morning." He leaned back, studying her as though attempting to decipher some unspoken thought.

The breakfast spread was generous—soft-boiled eggs, fresh-baked rolls, fruit preserves, and a rather enticing platter of smoked salmon. A waiter moved to pour Eleanor a cup of coffee. Nathaniel, without a word, took up the sugar bowl and passed it to her. His fingers brushed against hers—deliberate, fleeting, and enough to send a shiver up her spine.

She kept her expression neutral, though her heart betrayed her with an uneven rhythm. Instead, she busied herself with stirring her drink. "We have only today to solve this."

Nathaniel set his cup down. "We know the murderer is a highwayman—someone with a history of robbery. But they hid the mask with the brooch. Why?"

Eleanor frowned. "If the mask had been found in their possession, they would be exposed. But why not burn it? Why not destroy the evidence?"

"Perhaps they ran out of time. Maybe they never intended to kill Lady Genevieve."

Eleanor considering this, drummed her fingers against the table. "Alright, let us assume that she recognised them."

He nodded. "It makes sense. What if she discovered the highwayman's true identity and was planning to reveal it?"

"Or blackmail them. She was wearing the brooch when she was murdered, and then it disappeared. What if the theft of it has nothing to do with the murder? What if the person she was arguing with was the highwayman and when she threatened to blackmail him or her they decided to get rid of her and stole the broach to make it look like a theft gone wrong?"

"What of the poison? Death was clearly by blunt instrument, so who poisoned her and why?"

"And talking of it, where is the murder weapon? I haven't picked up any clues yet as to where it might be. Have you?"

He shook his head.

There was a brief silence between them as they both considered the implications. The breakfast room had begun to empty, the other guests making their way out to prepare for the final day of the game.

Eleanor sighed. "We need to think. Who among the guests has a past they've been careful to keep hidden? Who would risk everything if their secrets were exposed?"

Nathaniel tapped a finger against the table. "We also need to consider skill. Not everyone here could overpower Lady Genevieve, let alone execute a highwayman's kind of crime."

Eleanor glanced at the window, where winter's pale autumn light streamed into the room. "So, you think we are looking for a man?"

"I do."

"But what if a woman poisoned her, so that they could overpower her when she was weak?"

Nathaniel leaned forward. "Good point. You know we never followed up on the clue of the open window. I suggest when you have finished your breakfast that we go outside and see if we can spot anything."

*****

The morning was bright but bitterly cold, the kind of December day where the air was crisp and edged with frost. Robins hopped across the frostbitten grass, their red breasts vivid against the pale ground, while a thin veil of mist clung to the hedgerows. Eleanor pulled her coat tighter around her as she and Nathaniel stepped outside, and made their way around the Hall to the library window.

It came as no surprise to find the police had erected a makeshift barrier beneath the window, sectioning off the area with red and white striped tape.

"There's a distinct footprint," pointed out Nathaniel, "by the size of it, I would say it definitely belonged to a man's riding boot."

A ripple of teasing passed over Eleanor's face. "A woman might have put them on to fool us?"

He chuckled shaking his head at her. "Are you so determined the murderer is female?"

"It is at least possible."

"True."

"How do you know it is from a riding boot?"

He grinned. "I used to ride all the time. Do you see the indent there? Any riding boot should have a small tread and a heel that is about an inch high, which prevents the foot from sliding."

"Okay, I'm impressed. What size foot are you?"

"Ten."

"Do you think you could hover your foot over the print to ascertain if it is larger than your foot?"

He couldn't help grinning at her. "You better hold my arm so I don't fall on it and ruin the clue for everyone." Stepping as close to the tape as he could, he raised his right foot and hovered it inches above the print. "Can you see?"

Eleanor let go of his arm for a moment to bend down and better look.

"Hey!" Nathaniel wobbled.

Laughing, Eleanor jumped back up and steadied his arm as he brought his leg back over the barrier.

"The footprint is larger than your boot, but only just."

"We need to discover which guests brought riding boots with them."

"Yes, I agree. Riding boots at a hotel that doesn't have horses—quite a big clue. Maybe we can persuade one of the staff to cough up the information?"

Nathaniel caught sight of the morning light bouncing off Eleanor's rich brown hair creating a halo effect. A jolt went through him and he was overcome with a desire to kiss her again. "Eleanor, I..."

"I tell you, we've almost sussed it!"

They looked up to see the Leighton sisters approaching, arm in arm and heads bent together.

"Shush," hissed Emma Leighton.

"But it is true," Charlotte said, enthusiasm in her voice. "The only piece missing now is the weapon..." her voice trailed off as she caught sight of Nathaniel and Eleanor.

"Good morning, ladies," said Nathaniel.

"Morning," they echoed.

A few seconds of awkward silence fell between them. "We're just out for a stroll," declared Emma going bright red.

Eleanor smiled at her. "As are we. We will leave you to peruse the clue. Enjoy your morning." She linked her arm through Nathaniel's, and they set off for another walk around the stables.

"I shall concede, for the moment, that our culprit is a man," said Eleanor. "If that proves true, we may eliminate half the guests. Now we need only search among them for one with a foot larger than most. In this, we will hopefully discover the identity of our sixth suspect before anyone else does."

Nathaniel stroked his chin. "Let us think. Which of the gentlemen is tall?"

Eleanor tapped his arm with her gloved hand. "Lord Whitmore towers over you."

Nathaniel frowned. "I would not say towers."

She suppressed a smile. "Even so, I would wager his feet are larger than yours."

"Adam Beauchamp stands near my height, I believe."

Eleanor halted mid-step. "Adam!"

"Pardon?"

"The handkerchief! Genevieve held one embroidered with an 'A.' Adam! If his feet are larger than yours, then two clues point in his direction."

"The handkerchief—I took it as proof against Albert, which was why I felt certain of his guilt."

"I never noticed Adam among the actors. He has played his part well."

Nathaniel's expression darkened. "If indeed he plays one at all. We need proof."

"Let us leave the stable and the weapon for now. A loose-tongued servant may prove more useful in leading us to a particular pair of riding boots."

As if fate had heard them, no sooner had they stepped into Winterbourne Hall than they spied the butler, Mr Donald Grady, carrying silverware along the corridor.

"Sir, might we have a word?" Nathaniel called as they moved after him.

"I have much to do before luncheon is served," Mr Grady noted over his shoulder without breaking stride.

"Only a brief question, if you would."

At last, the butler halted. "And what might that be?"

Nathaniel took the lead. "Have you, by any chance, cleaned a pair of size eleven riding boots?"

The butler studied him with the measured patience of a man who had seen all manner of inquiries in his time. "Mr Blackwood, is it? I have been a butler all my life. I have cleaned more boots than I care to count."

Eleanor studied him keenly. Donald Grady had served at Winterbourne Hall for years, long before Mrs Winterbourne took possession of the estate. His presence here was as much a part of the house as the chandeliers or the faded tapestries in the great hall. Meeting his cool, pale gaze, she said, "What he means is, have you cleaned any this weekend."

At his hesitation, she pressed further. "If you cannot reveal that, perhaps you might shed light on the footprint outside the library window?"

His lips pressed together, a battle between duty and discretion waging within him. At last, with a sigh, he relented. "Aye, sir. Last evening. They were muddied, in a dreadful state, if I recall."

Eleanor couldn't bear the suspense. "To whom did they belong?"

Mr Grady cast a wary glance around before lowering his voice. "Lord Whitmore."

A flicker of triumph passed through Nathaniel's expression.

Eleanor released a slow breath. "Then we have our highwayman."

As Mr Grady resumed his duties, Eleanor and Nathaniel stood in silence, their gazes locked.

"He may not be the murderer, even if he is the highwayman," Nathaniel said.

"Then why was his footprint outside the library window?"

The game, the investigation, all of it faded from thought as Nathaniel stepped closer.

"Eleanor, there is something I wish to ask you."

She blinked, her voice failing her, every sense sharpened, waiting.

"When—"

"It's gone! It's been stolen!"

They turned sharply. Mrs Winterbourne stood unsteadily in the hallway, her face pale.

One swift glance passed between them before they rushed forward, Nathaniel reaching Beatrice just in time to catch her as she swooned.

*****

A shriek rang through the hall as Mrs Florence Colepepper spotted Mrs Winterbourne lying on the floor. Charging down the hallway, cooks pure white pinny swayed in the opposite direction of her skirts.

The exclamations of the gathered company faltered into silence as all turned out of various rooms to behold Mrs Winterbourne, who was coming around and moaning in unmistakable distress.

"It is gone!" she cried, pushing Nathaniel away and getting to her feet, her voice trembling with horror. "The Mistletoe Bauble has been stolen!"

For the space of a breath, no one moved. Then, with a dramatic sigh, Mrs Winterbourne's eyes fluttered shut, and she crumpled to the floor again in a heap of silken skirts.

A flurry of activity ensued. Mrs Poppy Hargreaves, ever the capable housekeeper, rushed forward, barking orders for smelling salts, while Mr Dunlop made an attempt—albeit a cautious one—to assist in reviving their hostess.

"She has swooned," declared Colonel Montague, folding his arms. "How very inconvenient."

Miss Emma Leighton, whose nerves seldom withstood such incidents, clutched at her sister. "But the game! We are on the cusp of discovery—this is quite the worst possible moment for a true crime to occur."

"Theft is a crime of the lowest sort," added Miss Charlotte, shaking her head. "Had it been a second murder, I should at least have had the satisfaction of being proved correct in my suspicions."

A murmur of agreement rippled through the guests, though whether they sympathised with the Leighton sisters or merely shared their frustration at this unexpected disruption was unclear.

Nathaniel touched Eleanor's arm. "The day takes an unexpected turn."

Eleanor, whose thoughts had already begun racing ahead, cast her gaze about the room. She and Nathaniel had scarcely finished whispering their latest revelation when the commotion had begun. Lord Whitmore's boots and the print outside the library. The highwayman's mask and stolen jewel.

A footman, having been dispatched with all urgency, now returned with the solemn announcement that the authorities had been summoned. He spoke to Mr Donald Grady's ear.

The butler stood straight. "Until their arrival," he said, assuming a position of temporary authority, "everyone is requested to wait in the Bluebell Parlour."

With several loud grumbles and a few comments of sympathy, everyone filed into the pretty room.

Colonel Montague harrumphed. "Imprisoned in a drawing-room like misbehaving schoolboys—preposterous."

Entering the room, Nathaniel took Eleanor's arm. "We must speak with Whitmore."

Eleanor did not disagree. A single glance confirmed that the gentleman in question was still in attendance, standing at the far end of the room, his expression unreadable.

"The question is," she said in a hushed tone, "how to reach him before every would-be detective in the room gets in our way or picks up on our interest in him."

It was no small challenge. Already, clusters of guests were beginning to form, each attempting to determine for themselves the sequence of events that had led to this most scandalous of thefts. "I've heard it is quite priceless," said one guest.

Lord Whitmore, as unruffled as ever, stood apart, one hand idly in his pocket.

Nathaniel took a step forward. Eleanor in tow.

But before they could so much as cross the room, a shrill voice interrupted their progress.

"This is most vexing," Miss Leighton lamented. "If we are to be detained, the least we can do is have the matter of Lady Genevieve's murder settled." She turned an accusatory glare upon Eleanor. "You, Miss Carstone, were there when Sophia made her revelation. What have you discovered?"

Eleanor, almost at a loss for words, opened her mouth to reply, but Nathaniel interceded with admirable swiftness.

"Patience is a virtue, Miss Leighton." He smiled, all politeness. "And though I know well your keen thirst for justice, I would remind you that the loss of the Mistletoe Bauble is, at present, the greater concern."

Miss Leighton sniffed. "That depends on whom you ask."

A stir near the doorway saved them from further argument. Mrs Winterbourne, now revived and fanning herself dramatically, was being assisted to a chair.

"The bauble," she said weakly. "It must be found."

"It will be, ma'am," Mrs Poppy Hargreaves assured her. "No one is to leave this room until the police have made their enquiries."

Eleanor exchanged a look with Nathaniel. They had only a short window of time before the authorities arrived and made private conversation impossible. "Quickly, before we lose him."

Determined, Eleanor and Nathaniel wove through the gathered guests, closing the distance between themselves and Lord Whitmore. He stood apart, posture easy, a faint air of disinterest about him as if the theft of the Mistletoe Bauble were but another weekend's diversion. His dark eyes flickered toward them as they approached, yet he did not move to greet them.

Nathaniel was the first to speak. "Lord Whitmore."

A slow nod was all he received in response.

Eleanor, ever the bolder of the two, asked, "I wonder, my lord, do you find yourself as surprised as the rest of us by this sudden turn of events?"

His lips quirked, but before he could reply, Sally swept past, pressing a glass of brandy into his hand with the easy familiarity of one accustomed to the task. "There you are, Ambrose," she said, before flitting away once more.

Eleanor stiffened. Ambrose. A.

Her eyes darted to Nathaniel's, and she saw her own realisation reflected back at her. A fresh tide of suspicion swelled.

Nathaniel smiled. "Ambrose," he echoed, watching closely. "A fine name."

A measured sip of brandy was Whitmore's only reply.

Eleanor folded her arms. "It is curious," she said, her tone deceptively light, "that you should bring riding boots to a hotel that does not have horses. Even more so that your boots should match a print left outside the library." It was a bluff, and she crossed her fingers behind her back.

This time, a flicker of something—mild surprise, perhaps—crossed Whitmore's features. "An accusation, Miss Carstone?"

Nathaniel interjected. "An observation."

A slow breath. A glance over their shoulders. Then Whitmore leaned in, lowering his voice just enough to ensure they alone would hear. "I admire your diligence. It is a rare pleasure to be questioned with such thoroughness."

Eleanor narrowed her eyes. "You play the part too well, my lord."

At that, Nathaniel, ever perceptive, seized the moment. "That is what you are, is it not?" he asked. "An actor?"

A pause.

Then, at last, a low chuckle. "I do my best."

The confession, though quiet, settled between them with a jolt of revelation. Of course. Whitmore—Ambrose—was one of Mrs Winterbourne's players. That much was clear. Yet clarity brought no resolution, for though they now knew him to be part of the grand deception, they still could not prove his involvement in the crime. The murder weapon remained missing.

Before she could press further, he straightened, offering them both a knowing smile. "This has been most diverting, but I believe you have had your fill of my company."

Eleanor bristled at the dismissal, but Nathaniel inclined his head with a good-natured air. "For now."

With that, they turned away, walking side by side, their heads inclined toward one another as they shared their findings in low tones. Their progress was halted, however, by the sound of Mr Donald Grady's measured voice cutting through the hum of conversation.

"The police have arrived."

All heads turned toward the butler, whose expression betrayed not the slightest hint of disturbance at the morning's events. He surveyed the assembled guests before adding, "The officers request volunteers for the first interviews."

Hardly had the words left his lips before Miss Emma Leighton and Miss Charlotte Leighton surged forward with matching cries of delight.

"Oh, us first!" Emma declared, seizing her sister's hand. "We should like to go together!"

"This is so thrilling," Charlotte added, her cheeks aglow.

Mr Grady, with his usual patience, gestured for them to proceed, and they swept into the adjoining room, their delight untempered by the gravity of the situation.

Eleanor, still preoccupied with thoughts of Whitmore, made her way over to a window seat, and sat on one of its lush cushions.

Nathaniel followed, leaning against the opposite side, watching her with an expression that suggested a thought had occurred to him. "If you had not been by my side all morning, I might have suspected you of taking the bauble."

Eleanor's head snapped up. "You *what?*"

Nathaniel, sensing danger, lifted his hands in mock surrender. "Only an observation. You have shown a great deal of interest in it, after all."

Eleanor stiffened, colour rising in her cheeks. "That is *preposterous.*"

And yet, her indignation wavered beneath the truth. She had, indeed, considered stealing the Mistletoe Bauble—not for herself, but to ensure it fell into the proper hands. A thought that had flickered at the weekend's beginning, before true complexity of the mystery had unfolded.

Nathaniel's eyes sharpened. "Eleanor…"

But she stood abruptly. "I have no idea what you mean."

Her avoidance did little to soothe his curiosity.

"Eleanor."

She turned away.

"Eleanor."

Still, she did not face him.

Nathaniel sighed, pushing himself from the window seat. "I did not mean to offend you."

She did not answer. Instead, she went to the far corner of the room, where the glow of the daylight from the tall paned-windows didn't reach. Arms crossed, she stared at nothing in particular, willing her vexation to subside.

Nathaniel, observing her for a long moment, shook his head. "Well," he muttered, mostly to himself, "that went well."

*****

Eleanor sat stiffly in the high-backed chair, arms folded, her gaze fixed on the polished surface of the desk before her. The room—one of Winterbourne Hall's smaller studies—had been repurposed as an impromptu interrogation room, and though the grandeur of the carved oak panels and antique furnishings remained, the presence of two uniformed officers made it far less distinguished.

Across from her, a broad-shouldered man in his fifties sat with a notepad balanced in his large hands. His short-cropped grey hair did nothing to soften his severe expression. Beside him, a younger officer, likely no older than thirty, flipped open a file and cleared his throat.

"Miss Eleanor Carstone," the younger officer began, his tone professional but clipped. "We understand you've taken quite an interest in the stolen item this weekend."

Under the table, Eleanor tugged at her sleeve. "As nothing more than a curiosity."

Detective Sergeant Sebastian Moffat lifted an unimpressed brow. "That's not what we've been told."

Eleanor raised her chin. "I don't know what you mean."

Moffat glanced at his colleague, who consulted his notes. "Mrs Winterbourne has informed us that you asked about the bauble multiple times, took a keen interest in its history, and even—" he turned a page, "—requested to see it up close."

Eleanor pressed her lips together. "I should imagine I was not the only guest who did so."

"Perhaps not," the younger officer allowed, flipping a page, "but you were the only guest who, according to the estate's caretaker, took more than a passing interest. More than once, he found you measuring up the locked display case. That's rather specific behaviour for someone who claims to be 'curious.'"

Eleanor's fingers stopped tugging at her cuff, worry causing her to still. "I wanted to understand the scale of it, that's all."

Moffat gave her a long, steady look. "Most people just admire through the glass."

Silence.

Eleanor's pulse hammered against her ribs.

Moffat leaned forward, clasping his hands together. "Would you like to explain why?"

She inhaled slowly, willing herself to remain calm. There was no avoiding the truth now. "I was hired by Mr Alistair Fenwick. He asked me to determine whether Mrs

112

Winterbourne's Christmas Bauble was the one stolen from his family's collection some twenty years ago."

Moffat's expression remained unreadable. "And what did you determine?"

"I informed them yesterday which of the five baubles Mrs Winterbourne had on display."

"And in your opinion, is it a stolen artefact?"

Eleanor met his gaze. "No. I am convinced it is the genuine ornament, properly returned to its rightful owner."

"So having done your job, why stay?"

A faint flush crept up Eleanor's neck. "I wanted to finish the murder mystery."

The officers exchanged a look that suggested they had heard flimsier excuses—but not many.

"You can see, I'm sure," Moffat said, his voice level, "why this makes you look rather suspicious. The bauble has been stolen, and we now have not one, but two witnesses who say you took an unusually strong interest in it."

Eleanor's jaw tightened. "And you think I would be foolish enough to take it after making my thoughts so publicly known?"

Moffat sniffed loudly. "You would be surprised."

Eleanor gritted her teeth. "Then let me be clear. I did not steal the bauble. I have no idea where it is."

The younger officer studied her for a moment before jotting something down. "Mr Grady confirms the item was in the glass cabinet at..." he checked his notes, "Ten. Mrs Winterbourne entered the ballroom at ten forty-five to discover it had been stolen. That is a forty-five minute window. Where were you at that time?"

"In the grounds. With Nathaniel Blackstone."

Moffat's pen stilled against the page. "Not in the house?"

Irritated. "No. As I said, I was outside."

The younger officer glanced up. "Can anyone else confirm that?"

Eleanor hesitated. "Besides Nathaniel you mean? No."

Moffat huffed, tapping his fingers once against his notebook. "So let's be clear: the bauble was taken this morning. We don't know when, but by the time the theft was discovered, you had been outside."

"Yes."

"And your only alibi is the man you've known for— what?—two days?"

Eleanor's fingers curled against the fabric of her skirt. "I understand how it looks. But I repeat... I did not steal it and at the time of theft I was outside."

Moffat shut his notebook. "Let's assume, for a moment, that's true. If you were in our position, Miss Carstone, who would *you* be looking at?"

Chapter 8

CLOSING THE BEDROOM DOOR with a quiet click, Eleanor leaned against it, letting out a long sigh. The interview had left her drained, her nerves frayed at the edges. The police had not accused her outright, but the suspicion in their eyes lingered like an unwelcome shadow. She pressed her fingers to her temples, willing herself to think—really think—about what had happened.

She had come here expecting to uncover a stolen artefact, only to find herself entangled in something far worse. And Nathaniel—Nathaniel had the audacity to accuse her, even in jest.

Pacing the room eased some of her tension until she felt calm enough to sit at the desk. The clock on her laptop showed 11:35. They were supposed to be dressed in Regency attire and in the dining room for 12:15. Would lunch still go ahead?

Poor Mrs Winterbourne! Eleanor dropped her head onto her arms. The woman loved that bauble so much. Who could have stolen it? An elaborate heist like this needed to be meticulously planned. The Hall brimmed over with people, to steal it in broad daylight knowing anyone could walk in on you at any moment—that took planning and precision. But who had the brains to pull that off?

A firm knock sounded at the door.

Eleanor stiffened. She knew who it was before he even spoke.

"Eleanor," came Nathaniel's voice, low and firm. "Let me in."

She closed her eyes. A refusal balanced on the tip of her tongue, but to leave him standing in the corridor would only invite further speculation. With a sharp inhale, she turned the latch and stepped back.

Nathaniel entered without hesitation, shutting the door behind him. The normal neatness of his appearance had given way to his frustration. His eyes searched hers, and whatever he saw there did not please him.

"You're still angry."

She folded her arms. "And you're not?"

Nathaniel let out a humourless laugh. "I am, actually. I'd thought, after everything, that you knew me better than to believe I meant that seriously."

Eleanor turned away, pacing toward the window. "You should have thought before you spoke."

"Oh, forgive me. I was unaware we were being held to such exacting standards."

She spun on her heels. "Do you think this is amusing?"

Nathaniel's jaw tightened. "No. I think it's ridiculous that you've spent all weekend hiding something from me, yet the moment I make a passing comment, you react as if I've actually accused you of theft."

"How do you know that?"

"After confirming your whereabouts, I came straight from my interview here. You forgot to mention the sisters can confirm our outdoor stroll. Moffat shared that little gem about your real reason to be here."

Though the electric heater poured forth ample warmth, a cold weight settled in her chest. She had hidden something from him. She had come here under false pretences, had intended—at least for a time—to steal the bauble herself.

Her hands clenched into fists.

He watched her, some of the anger fading from his expression. "Eleanor…"

"Okay, I admit it. I lied," she said abruptly. The words tasted bitter. "I didn't come here for the murder mystery."

Nathaniel didn't move. "I know."

She shook her head. "No, you don't. I came to steal the bauble. Not for myself, but to return it to the authorities."

A long silence stretched between them.

Nathaniel rubbed a hand down his face. "Well, that was unexpected."

"You said Moffat told you."

"He said you had been hired to check its authenticity."

"Oh."

"Oh, indeed."

A strained, breathless laugh escaped her. "That's all you have to say?"

"For the moment, yes." He studied her, something unreadable in his gaze. "Since we're being honest—" He hesitated, then squared his shoulders. "I lied as well."

Eleanor blinked.

"I'm not an author, at least, not of books." He paused and would have crossed his fingers if he believed in that kind of thing. "I'm a journalist. I came here to write an exposé on Mrs Winterbourne."

The room spun. Eleanor stared at him. "You—you're a journalist?"

"Yes."

Her stomach twisted. "And all this time—you've been watching, asking questions—"

"Not about you. I wasn't here for you, Eleanor. I didn't even know you would be here."

"But you were here to write about the guests, the weekend—about Mrs Winterbourne." Her breath hitched. "About me."

Nathaniel stepped closer. "Eleanor—"

He would have plenty to write about her now she had blurted out her secrets. "Get out."

He froze.

She shook her head, swallowing against the lump in her throat. "I trusted you."

"I never lied about the things that mattered."

She met his gaze, anger and betrayal warring in her chest. "I said, get out."

A muscle flickered in his jaw. For a moment, she thought he would argue. Then, without another word, he turned on his heel and left, shutting the door behind him.

Eleanor stood in the silence, hands trembling at her sides.

What had she done?

What had they both done?

*****

Eleanor must have dozed off briefly after she stopped crying, for she awoke to the sound of a faint tapping at the door. Opening it, she found Elizabeth, the chambermaid, standing there.

"Yes?"

"Miss Carstone, I am to inform you that lunch will proceed as scheduled. Please come down when you are ready."

"Must we still dress the part?"

"Mrs Winterbourne, given the recent circumstances, has said guests may attend as they wish."

"Thank you."

Elizabeth, still in character, curtsied and turned to knock on the next door.

Eleanor opened the wardrobe and, drawing out a simple pale pink dress of the softest muslin, mused aloud, "When will I ever get a chance to wear you? It is now or never." With this decision, she set about washing and dressing, pulling her hair into a soft bun, some brown curls left to frame her face. A tiny touch of rouge and a delicate smudge of pale pink lipstick were sufficient. She was ready.

As she descended the grand staircase, Donald Grady struck a small brass gong, announcing the commencement of lunch. She joined the guests making their way into the dining room, yet she could not help but search for Nathaniel, though he was nowhere to be seen. Disappointed, she made her way to her usual seat.

Lacking manners, and with little regard for kindness, most of the guests did not attempt to conceal their discussions, which centred on her as the probable thief of the bauble. She raised her chin and accepted a glass of white wine. Even Mrs Winterbourne would not acknowledge her, and inwardly, Eleanor began to falter.

"I didn't steal it!" she blurted, her voice rising with conviction.

A lady to her right sniffed and tossed her head. "Well, you are not likely to confess all over the roast, are you?"

"I didn't do it."

At last, Mrs Winterbourne noted the distress in Eleanor's voice and regarded her.

"I didn't take it, Mrs Winterbourne. I promise you."

"I hope not, my dear. I truly do. But as yet, we have no idea what has become of it."

Waiters arrived with pumpkin soup, and for a while, conversation regarding the theft ceased. Eleanor kept glancing at the empty chair beside her and soon concluded that Nathaniel must have left.

Finding her appetite lost, she pushed her soup aside. The waiter, seeing her bowl nearly untouched, asked, "Was the soup not to your liking, my lady?"

Eleanor flushed crimson as all eyes turned to her. "It was delicious, thank you. I am simply not overly hungry."

The stares faded as the guests returned to their private conversations, leaving Eleanor to her thoughts and solitude.

Platters of roast beef and vegetables were placed on the table, and the guests encouraged to help themselves. Eleanor took but the smallest portion of everything only longing for an escape.

Still chewing a mouthful of beef, Colonel Montague addressed no one in particular. "How much is that damned bauble worth? The thief has certainly put a dampener on matters. A most inconsiderate act—like a Jack Frost icing all our friendships with suspicion."

A gentleman at the far end of the table raised his fork. "The item, my friend, is priceless."

"Priceless," said Emma and Charlotte in unison.

"The value lies not in the materials, but in its history. A royal gift finds its place in the history books and becomes, therefore, priceless."

Mrs Dunlop dabbed at her mouth with her napkin. "Then why steal it?"

"My dear lady, some people possess more money than sense. They purchase such antiquities, only to hide them in their cellars, robbing the world of their brilliance," replied the distant guest.

Mr Dunlop waved a gloved hand dismissively. "How fascinating it is that so many historical artefacts vanish without a trace, no doubt sitting in private collections, unappreciated. I am not certain why anyone would covet a collection of Christmas baubles, though. There must be plenty of valuables more worthy of stealing in Devon."

Mrs Fairfax raised an eyebrow, mischief glinting in her eyes. "Oh, Mr Dunlop, you sound remarkably well-informed! Pray, have you been to Willowcombe Village before? Or are you secretly one of those treasure hunters one reads about?"

Mr Dunlop let out a short laugh, adjusting his cuffs. "Alas, Mrs Fairfax, I fear my life has been far less adventurous than that. No, I've never had the pleasure of visiting Willowcombe before this weekend." He took a measured sip of wine before adding, "However, I do keep myself well-read. *Antiquities & Curios, The Collector's Gazette…* one picks up all sorts of fascinating details in such esteemed publications."

Mrs Fairfax leaned her head to the side. "Indeed? If you have time later, I would be delighted to spend awhile talking with you about such things. It is seldom that one meets such an educated man."

Mrs Dunlop snorted. "Educated, is he? Well, that's news to me! He may read those magazines cover to cover, Mrs Fairfax, but the only thing he ever remembers is the price tags."

Laughter rippled around the table as Mr Dunlop gave his wife a wounded look. "That is *entirely* untrue."

Mrs Dunlop patted his hand. "Of course it is, dear."

Noticing Mr Dunlop's immaculate white gloves, Colonel Montague tugged his off and slapped them onto the table. "I say, old chap, how do you manage to eat with your gloves on? I cannot handle cutlery whilst wearing them. Impossible."

Mr Dunlop straightened, clearly taking the comment as a compliment. "When my dear wife first dragged me along to one of these Regency affairs, I came screaming and kicking like a petulant child. However, I have since grown accustomed to the attire—and the whole affair," he swept his arm wide, encompassing their surroundings. "I have come to believe I was born in the wrong era."

Laughter rippled down the table.

Adam Beauchamp, who had already removed his gloves, joined in. "I daresay, had you lived in the eighteen hundreds, when less than five per cent of the population was wealthy, you would have been born a pauper and would consider yourself most unfortunate for not being born in the twenty-first century."

Laughter erupted once more, with many agreeing.

Eleanor was pushing her honey-roasted parsnip around her plate when movement at the far side of the dining room caught her eye. She looked up. Nathaniel strode across the room, his presence as infuriating as it was—no, she would not complete that thought. Instead, she forced herself to appear wholly unaffected and returned to prodding her food as though it held the answers to all life's mysteries.

"Do you mind?" Nathaniel asked, placing his hands on the back of the empty chair beside her.

"By all means."

As he pulled out the chair, a waiter materialised at his side. "My lord, would you care for a portion of soup?"

"No, thank you. I shall tuck into this wonderful roast before me."

The waiter bowed and withdrew, only for Mr Grady to appear with the decanter. Nathaniel lifted his glass obligingly.

"Thank you. That is enough."

The butler gave a brisk nod and stepped away.

"You are late, in a most ill-mannered fashion."

"Ha! The lady speaks to me. How gratified I should be."

She dropped her fork onto her plate with an unceremonious clang. Several nearby guests turned their heads. "You should have stayed away."

"What, and miss this feast? Never." He proceeded to help himself to generous portions of roast beef, potatoes, and green beans, utterly unbothered by her glare.

She leaned in, lowering her voice. "Your appetite seems insatiable. How can you sit here, enjoying Mrs Winterbourne's hospitality, while planning to stab her in the back?"

Nathaniel stiffened. "Eleanor—"

She shoved her chair back, prepared to leave. Before she could rise, his hand settled firmly on her knee beneath the table. Not forceful, but insistent.

She stiffened, hissing under her breath, "What are you doing?"

"Saving you from further embarrassment. Stay, behave, and listen. I have something of importance to share."

Eleanor folded her arms, torn between indignation and curiosity. "Unless it's a full-page apology in tomorrow's papers, I am not interested."

Nathaniel sighed, reaching for his glass. "What if I told you I have already spoken with the dear lady and begged her forgiveness?"

She narrowed her eyes. "You did?"

"Well. Not yet." He took a measured sip of wine before adding, "But if you work with me on this, I give you my word I will."

Eleanor hesitated, searching his face for any sign of deception. "What is 'this' exactly?"

Nathaniel set down his glass and shifted closer, his voice pitched for her ears alone. "I believe I've found something that will solve the murder."

She arched a brow. "You mean the game? I am otherwise occupied with a real crime."

"So am I. And I think they're connected." He tapped his fork against his plate. "I've spent the last two hours researching Winterbourne House."

Eleanor gave a sceptical hum, though her pulse quickened.

"Seventy years ago," Nathaniel continued, "an article was published about the history of the estate. It mentions something rather intriguing—secret passageways."

She drew back. "That would be fitting for the setting of a murder mystery."

He nodded. "More than fitting—it explains something that's been bothering me since we found that single footprint outside the library window."

Eleanor frowned. "Go on."

"The footprint faces the window, as though the killer entered from outside. But there was no second print leading away." He took another bite of food before adding, "Which means, if my theory is correct, the murderer didn't leave the way they came in."

Her grip tightened on her napkin. "You think there's a passageway in the library?"

Nathaniel's eyes gleamed. "I think there might be. And if there is—"

"Then that is where the murder weapon is hidden."

His smile was full of mischief. "Precisely."

The idea was ludicrous. Preposterous. The kind of thing that belonged in the pages of a novel.

And yet.

She glanced around the table. No one was paying them any mind now, more concerned with their own speculations about the game and the theft of the bauble.

She turned back to Nathaniel. "If I agree to help you, you will apologise to Mrs Winterbourne?"

"I swear on my professional integrity."

"I rather thought you had none."

Nathaniel pressed a hand to his chest in mock injury. "Wounding."

She let out a long breath. "Fine. We finish lunch. Then we search the library."

His grin widened. "I knew you would see sense."

She picked up her fork and stabbed the parsnip with unnecessary force. "Just don't make me regret it."

*****

Nathaniel ran his hands along the panelled wall, pressing lightly, listening intently. "There must be something. Old houses like this don't just lose their secrets."

Eleanor, standing a few feet away, with a gentle touch dragged her fingertips over the ornate carvings of the bookshelf, searching for any irregularity. "We're assuming it hasn't been sealed up years ago. We might be chasing ghosts."

He shot her a look. "Or we might be chasing answers."

She huffed but kept searching, tapping experimentally at the wooden panelling. The sound was solid, unyielding.

Nathaniel took a step back, surveying the room. "If I were a secret passage, where would I be?"

Before Eleanor could reply, the door creaked open. In an instant, she snatched a book from the shelf, flipping it open as though she had been engrossed in it all along. Nathaniel did the same, adopting an expression of thoughtful interest.

"Ah, Miss Carstone, Mr Blackstone." Harold Harcourt strolled into the library. "How industrious you both look. Planning to enlighten us all with your newfound wisdom?"

Eleanor smiled thinly, snapping her book shut. "We were discussing a theft."

Harcourt's brows lifted. "The bauble?"

"No," Nathaniel said, slipping his book back onto the shelf. "The copy of *Northanger Abbey* that has gone missing."

Harcourt let out a short laugh. "I should think that's hardly a theft worthy of discussion. Probably some young lady wishing to impress, 'But for my own part, if a book is well written, I always find it too short.' Some such quote will be bandied around for grandiloquent effect. No doubt it will mysteriously appear on the day the guests depart."

Nathaniel glanced at Eleanor before replying. "You don't find it peculiar, considering the events of the weekend?"

"Nothing about this weekend has been remotely ordinary," Harcourt barked, selecting a book for himself. "But I fail to see how a missing novel warrants suspicion."

Nathaniel pressed on. "The book, the moving furniture in the study... It all seems rather deliberate, wouldn't you say?"

Harcourt chuckled. "My dear fellow, if we paused to examine every peculiarity, we might never finish our brandy."

With that, he retreated to an armchair by the fire, leaving Nathaniel and Eleanor to exchange a glance.

Eleanor rolled her eyes. "He's not going anywhere."

"Typical," Nathaniel sighed. He leaned against the bookcase, lowering his voice. "Regardless, the book and the study—I can't shake the feeling they're connected."

Eleanor frowned, fingers idly running along the spines of the books. "You think someone moved the furniture to look for something?"

"Or to hide something."

A chill passed over her. "Like the bauble?"

"Or the murder weapon."

Then, as if summoned by their discussion, the door opened once more. They both straightened stiffly, eyes turning innocently to the shelves.

Mrs Fairfax strode in, gaze sweeping the room before landing on Harcourt. "There you are! I require your opinion on a matter of grave importance."

Harcourt sighed, setting his book aside. "If I must."

As soon as the door clicked shut behind them, Nathaniel let out a breath. "Finally."

Eleanor shot him a look. "Let's make good use of the time before the next interruption."

And, without another word, they returned to their search.

Eleanor stood at the far end of the library, fingers trailing along the spines of well-worn books, her mind only half-aware of the titles. Nathaniel, across the room, rapped his knuckles lightly against the panelled wall, pausing after each knock as if expecting a hollow echo to betray the passage they sought.

"You could at least pretend to be interested in the books," she muttered, eyes flitting to the door.

"I am interested. Just not in the manner expected."

She sighed and withdrew a volume at random. *A Treatise on the Agricultural Improvements of the Late Eighteenth Century.* She grimaced. "Not exactly riveting."

Nathaniel smirked. "I'm sure it's an excellent cure for insomnia."

Eleanor considered the mystery of the misplaced furniture had been dismissed as a guest's idle whimsy, but the theft of *Northanger Abbey*—a novel about secrets, suspicion, and mistaken identities—felt more deliberate. But for the life of her she couldn't connect the dots.

A silence stretched between them as they searched.

Then, the door creaked open once more. Eleanor and Nathaniel instantly straightened, their gazes turning innocently to the shelves.

Miss Emma Leighton swept in with a decisive air, her keen gaze scanning the room before settling on the would be bookworms. "You don't fool me, you're looking for the murder weapon are you not. Charlotte and I have searched the room thoroughly, you will not find it here."

"From one straight talker to another, Miss Leighton," said Nathaniel, "if that is the case why, may I ask, are you here?"

"I am looking for my sister."

Nathaniel gestured around the room. "As you can see, she is not here. Unless she's hiding under the desk. Miss Charlotte, yoo-hoo, are you there?"

"Don't be ridiculous," snapped Emma spinning around and leaving with a loud huff.

Nathaniel grinned. "Finally."

Eleanor shot him a pointed look. "Let's make good use of the time before the *next* interruption."

Nathaniel was already moving, running his hands along the panelled wall again, pressing at the carved wood with deliberate precision.

Eleanor, watching him, felt a flicker of impatience. "We're going about this the wrong way." She stepped back and studied the room as a whole. "If this house has secret passageways, they wouldn't be hidden at random. There would be logic to it—an entrance placed somewhere discreet but accessible. Somewhere an intruder could slip in and out unseen. Where did they go?"

Nathaniel scanned the walls again before his eyes fell on the towering bookshelf nearest the fireplace. "There, if I were a secret passage, that's where I would be."

Eleanor followed his gaze, studying the bookcase. "But how do we—"

Nathaniel was already reaching for the books, pressing experimentally along the spines. Eleanor did the same, running her fingers along the carved edges of the shelves.

And then—

A faint click.

Eleanor froze. She had felt it, beneath her fingertips—a book that shifted with resistance and then left something that could be a latch beneath her touch.

She met Nathaniel's gaze, excitement sparking between them.

"Do it," he urged.

Eleanor held her breath and pulled the catch. There was a moment of resistance, then another click, deeper this time.

With a soft groan, the entire bookcase trembled, then eased forward an inch. A thin, dark line appeared along the edge where the shelves met the wall.

Nathaniel placed both hands against the frame and pushed. The bookcase swung open, revealing a narrow passage beyond—dark, musty, and lined with aged stone. A draught of cool air wafted from the hidden space, carrying the scent of dust and secrets long undisturbed.

Eleanor swallowed. "Well, that is definitely a secret passageway."

Nathaniel grinned. "Shall we?"

Before they could step inside, footsteps sounded in the corridor outside.

"I tell you," said Emma, her voice carrying through the heavy wooden door, "they're looking for the murder weapon. What if we missed something and they find it?"

Eleanor's heart leapt into her throat.

"Quickly!" She slipped into the passageway with Nathaniel right behind her. Together, they pulled the panel closed just as Charlotte replied,

"Alright, as you wish. Let's check on them."

The panel clicked shut an instant before the library door swung open.

Chapter 9

THE AIR IN THE PASSAGE was thick with dust, disturbed only by their careful footsteps. Nathaniel moved ahead, his phone's torch held high, casting long, flickering shadows on the stone walls. The passage was so narrow they could barely move in single file. Every time Eleanor stepped aside to let Nathaniel examine something, she brushed against the rough chill of ancient stones.

She ran a hand along the wall, her fingers coming away smeared with dust—except in places where it had already been disturbed. Someone had been here.

Nathaniel turned, his breath warm in the confined space. "Look at this." He crouched and pointed his torch at the floor. The dust lay in uneven patches, as though someone had moved through recently and unthinkingly left a trail. "Not exactly footprints, but something—or someone—has been through here."

Eleanor nodded. "This must be how the murderer got away unseen."

He nodded and pushed forward, following the passage as it took a gradual turn. The air grew slightly warmer, carrying the faint scent of polished wood and candle wax. Then, at last, they reached a narrow wooden door, blending seamlessly with the surrounding stone. Nathaniel pressed against it, and with a soft creak, it swung open a fraction.

Peering through the gap, Eleanor's pulse raced. A grand chandelier glowed above, its golden light spilling onto polished parquet floors. The hushed murmur of voices drifted across the room from the hall.

"The ballroom!" Nathaniel turned to her, eyes alight with revelation. "This must be how the thief entered the ballroom without being seen."

"Then that means…" She trailed off, staring into the grand room beyond. The thief had been hiding in Winterbourne Hall all along.

Eleanor pulled the door shut as carefully as she could, heart still hammering from their discovery. They stood in the dim passageway, the sound of the ballroom and the house muffled once more by the thick wooden panel.

"Well," Nathaniel breathed, turning the light on his phone back on. "That explains how the thief escaped with the bauble although not how he managed to open and lock the cabinet, or who took it."

Eleanor leaned back against the cold stone wall. "It has to be someone who knew about this passageway. Someone who could slip away unnoticed, use it to enter the ballroom, steal the Mistletoe Bauble, and vanish again without a trace."

Nathaniel nodded. "Which means it's likely one of the guests."

They stood for a moment, considering the implications. Just beyond this hidden door, their fellow guests—dressed in Regency finery for the last time—were mingling, sipping fruit punch, and making their final murder mystery accusations. Any one of them could be the thief.

"And yet, we still don't know where the murder weapon is. The poker was never recovered. If we found that, we might find our thief."

Nathaniel rubbed his chin. "Alright, let's think. We know where the murder took place—Genevieve was found in the library. We know where the bauble was taken—the ballroom. Could the two be connected?"

133

Eleanor frowned. "You mean the poker might have been hidden somewhere along this passage?"

"Possibly," Nathaniel said, glancing back down the narrow corridor. "We didn't check every inch of it. But more likely, if the thief used this passageway, they wouldn't risk leaving the weapon here. They would want it somewhere easy to retrieve, in case they needed to dispose of it later."

Eleanor bit her lip. "But where? If they were smart, they would have hidden it somewhere people wouldn't think to look. Somewhere... unexpected."

Nathaniel's eyes gleamed. "Somewhere that fits with the setting."

Understanding dawned. "What if... what if they hid it in plain sight? Among the fire pokers in one of the drawing rooms?"

Nathaniel let out a low whistle. "That would be clever. Who would question a poker sitting by a fireplace?"

"Then we need to check before the game ends. If we're right, we might find the missing weapon—and the person who planted it."

Nathaniel grinned. "Then what are we waiting for? Let's go."

With one last glance at the hidden door, they turned and hurried back through the passage, ready to make their final move.

*****

Eleanor cracked open the library door and peered inside. The room was empty, just as they had left it. The fire still

134

smouldered in the hearth, casting a warm flickering glow over the tall bookshelves and the gleam of polished furniture.

"All clear," she said, stepping inside. Nathaniel followed, closing the door behind them.

She crossed to the fireplace, her gaze drawn to the iron stand beside the hearth. Shovel. Brush. Tongs.

She frowned.

"Something wrong?"

Eleanor leaned in closer. "The poker. It's missing."

Nathaniel moved beside her, scanning the stand. "Are you sure there was one here?"

"There should be." She gestured at the stand. "It's part of a set. And it makes sense, doesn't it? If the murderer used it, it had to come from here."

Nathaniel rubbed his jaw. "Which means it was never found because they hid it too well for the guests to find."

They stood in silence, the crackling of the fire the only sound between them. Then Nathaniel turned and leaned against the edge of the desk.

"Alright," he said. "Let's go over what we know. One— Lady Genevieve was murdered."

Eleanor nodded. "Two—whoever played the murderer stole her brooch and hid it in the stables with the highwayman's mask."

Nathaniel tapped his fingers against the desk. "Three—on the night she was murdered, she was discussing highwaymen with someone. And there was an article about highwaymen in her room."

Eleanor frowned. "Four—the embroidered handkerchief with the letter 'A' on it."

135

Nathaniel held up a fifth finger. "And she was seen arguing with someone near the stables the day we arrived."

Eleanor chewed her lip. "Six—we now know there was a sixth actor involved in the game. And we've ruled out three of the remaining suspects—Leo Vaunt, Albert Wellington, and Sophia De'Luciosi. That leaves three people. Angela. Sally. And…" Her voice trailed off as realisation struck.

Nathaniel blinked and sat up straight. "Ambrose."

Eleanor turned to him, nodding. "Ambrose Whitmore is more than an actor."

Nathaniel let out a low whistle. "The highwayman."

"The murderer," Eleanor whispered.

They stared at each other, the pieces clicking into place.

Nathaniel pushed off the desk. "So if he's our culprit, that still leaves one question."

"Where did he hide the poker?"

Eleanor turned to face the window. Outside, the winter afternoon was beginning to darken, casting long shadows across the lawn. In the distance, the stables stood silent.

A thought stirred in her mind. The poker was taken from the library. The brooch and mask were hidden in the stables. What if…

She turned to Nathaniel. "If he wanted to hide the poker, he wouldn't have risked carrying it far. But he also wouldn't have left it somewhere obvious."

Nathaniel followed her gaze. "Somewhere between here and the stables?"

Eleanor nodded. "If the guests were meant to find it, but no one has, then maybe it's somewhere just hidden enough to go unnoticed." She hesitated. "Halfway between here and the stables… What if it was buried?"

Nathaniel stood up. "Let's grab our coats and go find it."

Without another word, they slipped from the library and raced upstairs, side-by-side. Minutes later, they stepped out into the cold in search of the final piece of the puzzle.

*****

The cold bit at Eleanor's cheeks as she walked over the frost-hardened ground, the crunch of her boots the only sound besides the distant whistle of wind. The sky darkened further, the low winter sun casting long, eerie shadows across the lawn.

Nathaniel walked beside her, eyes scanning the ground. "If he buried it, he wouldn't have gone too deep. Not if the guests were supposed to find it."

Eleanor nodded, wrapping her arms around herself. "It has to be somewhere someone might have stumbled upon if they had been paying attention."

They were about halfway between the library and the stables when Nathaniel suddenly stopped.

"Here."

Eleanor turned and followed his gaze. The earth just ahead of them was uneven, a patch of ground subtly raised, the soil darker than the rest.

She crouched down, running her fingers lightly over the surface. It had been disturbed—recently. "It's been dug up and patted back down."

Nathaniel straightened. "Wait here."

He strode to the stables, boots crunching against the frozen path. Eleanor rose and watched as he disappeared inside. Moments later, he emerged, carrying a spade. The blade was caked in mud—fresh mud, not the dry, crumbling kind that would suggest it had been there for years.

He held it up for her to see. "Looks like someone was digging not too long ago."

She grinned. "Let's find out what they hid."

Nathaniel drove the spade into the earth. The soil, though damp, was not fully frozen, making it easy to shift. He worked like a man on a mission, digging deeper with each thrust of the blade. Eleanor crouched beside him, hands hovering, ready to help.

Then—clang.

Nathaniel froze. He dug a little more before reaching down, fingers closing around something solid. He pulled it from the earth.

The missing poker!

Its iron shaft was streaked with dirt, but what caught Eleanor's eye was something else—something caught around the handle. A scrap of fabric, torn and tangled.

She reached out and carefully pulled it free. It was dark, richly coloured. As she turned it in the fading light, she caught the faint shimmer of gold embroidery along one edge and a waft of lemon.

Her breath hitched.

She looked up at Nathaniel. His eyes met hers, widening as the same realisation struck him.

"This…" Eleanor's fingers tightening around the fabric. "This came from Ambrose's coat and I can smell his lemon cologne too." She gripped the scrap of fabric tightly. They had found the poker, found proof that Ambrose had hidden it—but what now?

She turned to Nathaniel. "How long do we have before the game ends?"

He pulled his pocket watch from his waistcoat and flipped it open. "Thirty minutes."

Eleanor released a sharp breath. "That's not long. Nice watch, by the way."

Nathaniel grinned. "I thought it added a certain je ne sais quoi to my attire."

With a nod, he bent to retrieve the poker. "We had better get this inside."

"Wait." She reached out, pressing a hand against his arm. "We're supposed to leave the clues where we find them, remember? We have to leave it here."

Nathaniel swore under his breath and let the poker drop back into the hole with a dull thud. "You're right." He straightened, brushing dirt from his hands. "Then let's get away from here before someone sees us and puts two and two together."

He shovelled some of the mud back over the poker and the two of them patted the soil down with their feet trying not to laugh.

Without another word, they returned the spade to its place in the stable and hurried back to the house. Snowflakes fell heavy and thick, swirling in the air around them. Laughing, they raced hand-in-hand up the cobbled path back to the house.

They reached the terrace steps just as the great doors swung open and a pair of guests stepped outside, laughing over some last-minute theory about the murder mystery. Eleanor and

Nathaniel slowed their pace, schooling their expressions into ones of casual indifference.

With carefully measured steps, they climbed the stairs and slipped back into the warmth of Winterbourne Hall.

*****

An expectant air of silence filled the library, broken only by the occasional rustle of fabric as guests shifted in their seats. The fire crackled in the hearth, its warmth casting flickering shadows over the assembled crowd. Mrs Winterbourne stood before them, poised and elegant as ever, though a touch of weariness lined her features.

"Ladies and gentlemen," she began, her voice carrying easily through the room, "before we bring this most marvellous weekend to a close, I wish to express my gratitude. Your participation in this event has not only brought life to Winterbourne Hall but has also contributed to its future.

"This house was in my family for generations before it was lost to us. Being able to reclaim it two years ago was a dream come true, but restoring it is an ongoing endeavour. Thanks to your generous support, I will be able to continue with the renovations, ensuring that Winterbourne Hall stands for many more years to come."

A polite round of applause rippled through the guests, a few nodding in agreement.

"But," she continued with a gleam of mischief in her eye, "we are not quite finished yet. You still have one final task. On the last page of your notebooks, I ask you to write down the name of the murderer, the weapon, its location, your proof, and the motive. Mr Grady will collect them shortly, and then we shall see who among you has the sharpest mind for mystery."

A murmur of excitement spread through the room as guests flipped open their notebooks and put pen to paper. Eleanor felt excited as she scribbled down her answers:

Murderer: Lord Ambrose Whitmore

Weapon: The fireplace poker

Location: Buried outside, near the stable

Proof: A piece of Ambrose's jacket on the murder weapon

Motive: Genevieve was blackmailing him

She hesitated for only a second before closing the notebook with a quiet snap. Beside her, Nathaniel had already finished, his expression unreadable.

Across the room, the butler, Mr Grady, moved efficiently from guest to guest, gathering up their completed books. When the last one was placed in his hands, he carried them over to Mrs Winterbourne, who, along with him, began the task of scanning each entry.

The tension in the room was palpable, the only sounds being the flicking of pages and the occasional raised eyebrow from Mrs Winterbourne.

Finally, she lifted her gaze and smiled. "I must say, I am quite impressed. Many of you correctly identified our culprit as Lord Ambrose Whitmore."

A light round of applause sounded. Lord Whitmore, seated near the fireplace, gave a theatrical sigh and spread his hands as if to say, Alas, you have caught me!

"But," Mrs Winterbourne continued, "only one among you has managed to locate the murder weapon and correctly identify the proof."

A ripple of curiosity swept through the guests. Eleanor felt her heart pick up pace.

She turned a little as Mrs Winterbourne's gaze settled on her. "Miss Carstone, it would seem you have bested us all."

A small gasp ran through the crowd before applause burst forth, warm and congratulatory. Eleanor felt her cheeks heat as she dipped her head in acknowledgment. Nathaniel leaned in and murmured, "You do enjoy making a spectacle of yourself, don't you?"

"Hush," she whispered back, though she couldn't quite suppress a smile.

Mrs Winterbourne gestured toward Lord Whitmore. "Now, if you would, my lord, do tell us how it was done."

Lord Whitmore stood with a flourish, straightening his cravat as if preparing for a stage performance. "Ah, the sweet thrill of deception! Ladies and gentlemen—allow me to confess my wickedness."

The guests chuckled as he strode to the centre of the room. "Lady Genevieve and I had a rather… spirited conversation about highwaymen, which, of course, was all part of the grand charade. But in truth, Genevieve had dirt on me—rather embarrassing dirt, I might add."

A few guests exchanged knowing glances.

"After recognising my voice on the day we arrived, she blackmailed me, demanding an outrageous sum to keep her silence. And, as any reasonable rogue would do, I opted for murder instead!" He pressed a dramatic hand to his chest before grinning.

A slow turn of the room showed him that he held everyone's attention.

"A slow death by just the right amount of poison seemed a good way to dispense of her. Imagine how irritated I became when I heard her whisper to Leo Vaunt to meet her in the library in fifteen minutes. I couldn't allow her to share her information, so I slipped out first and waited for her there. When she entered, I retrieved the fireplace poker and dispatched dear Genevieve with one decisive blow."

He mimed the action with exaggerated flair.

"I was about to leave back through the window when I heard someone approaching, I hid behind the curtain. When the chambermaid went running off to find Mrs Winterbourne, I dropped the poker out of the window and calmly walked back to the ballroom. Using the time you were all called into the library I slipped outside, retrieved the poker and buried it.

"Later that night, I couldn't sleep due to worry about my identity. As you know, I stole the brooch as a misdirection for motive. When everyone, nearly everyone, went to bed," he winked at Eleanor, "I went back to the stable and hid the damming evidence. And ta-da, there you have it. What a dreadful bloke I am! I have to say, Miss Carstone, I am quite impressed you found it."

Eleanor dipped her head again, satisfaction warming her chest, she turned as if to speak and include Nathaniel but he shook his head.

Mrs Winterbourne clapped her hands once. "Well, there we have it! Thank you, Lord Whitmore, for that most entertaining confession. And congratulations once more to Miss Carstone, who has won our grand prize—an all-expenses-paid week's stay at Winterbourne Hall."

The guests broke into enthusiastic applause once more, and Eleanor found herself laughing softly.

Nathaniel leaned in. "Well done, Sherlock. How do you feel about another week in this grand old house?"

"As long as no one gets murdered, I think I shall quite enjoy it."

Mrs Winterbourne smiled warmly at the gathered guests. "And with that, my dear friends, I invite you all to celebrate the conclusion of our mystery weekend with a final glass of Champagne before you depart."

There was a general hum of approval, guests beginning to chatter excitedly about what marvellous fun the whole weekend had been.

Eleanor glanced at Nathaniel. They had solved the mystery game, but the heist had yet to be unravelled.

But for now, at least, the game was over.

*****

The hum of conversation filled the room as guests sipped their final glasses of Champagne. The fire crackled in the hearth, casting a golden glow over the assembled company. Laughter rippled from a corner where a small group reminisced about the weekend's more dramatic moments—false accusations, hasty deductions, and, of course, the grand reveal of the murderer.

Eleanor stood near the window, swirling the last of her drink, letting the bubbles dance against her lips as she glanced around. The room had taken on that particular air of an event drawing to a close—warm, contented, but with a hint of melancholy. And yet, her own mind was anything but settled.

A familiar voice interrupted her thoughts.

"Miss Carstone."

She turned to find Mrs Winterbourne beside her, an unreadable expression on her face.

"Have you given any thought to when you might return for your free week?"

Eleanor hesitated. She had assumed Mrs Winterbourne would want time to consider whether she could trust her, especially with the Mistletoe Bauble still missing. But if she was asking…

"Actually, would it be possible for me to stay this week?" Eleanor ventured, her fingers tightening around the stem of her glass.

Mrs Winterbourne regarded her carefully. "That depends."

Eleanor swallowed. "On?"

"On whether or not you stole my bauble."

The words were spoken without malice, but they pressed down on Eleanor's chest all the same.

"And do you believe I did?" she asked, keeping her voice steady.

Mrs Winterbourne's gaze drifted over the crowd before returning to Eleanor. "Only half… which, I must say, is quite the improvement."

Eleanor let out a breath she hadn't realised she was holding.

"Fortunately," Mrs Winterbourne continued, "I have only six guests next week, and therefore have spare rooms. You would be welcome to extend your visit with us."

Eleanor felt warmth bloom in her chest. "Then I'd be delighted to stay."

Mrs Winterbourne gave a small, satisfied nod before moving on to speak with other guests. Eleanor watched her go, a strange mixture of relief and apprehension settling over her.

She was staying. But that didn't mean she was in the clear just yet. The police had already asked for another interview with her tomorrow.

"You look as though you've been given a death sentence," Nathaniel said from behind her.

She turned to find him watching her, his own Champagne untouched.

"Not quite," she said. "More of a suspended sentence."

Nathaniel smirked. "So you're staying?"

"I am." Then, after a pause, "And what about you? It's time to fulfil your promise and speak with Mrs Winterbourne."

He held up a hand. "Already taken care of. I have an appointment with her in the morning."

Eleanor blinked. "In the morning? You mean—you're staying another night?"

His lips quirked. "Another week, actually."

Her breath caught. She had been prepared for a witty retort, for some flippant remark, but not that.

"A week?" she echoed.

"I've already booked my room."

Despite herself, Eleanor felt heat rise to her cheeks.

She forced lightness into her tone. "And is that to complete your article, or…?"

Nathaniel's eyes glinted. "Now, that is the real mystery, isn't it?"

Eleanor huffed, taking a sip of her Champagne to hide the way her pulse had quickened.

Somehow, she suspected that question would linger far longer than the weekend itself.

*****

Unable to sleep, Eleanor slipped out of bed, pulled on her dressing gown, and crept downstairs. Turning left at the bottom, she made her way to the morning room.

After switching on the light, she walked over to the John Broadwood & Sons piano, admiring its simple yet elegant style. Too delicate to play anymore, Beatrice had covered the top with family photographs in various frames. A part of Eleanor felt like she was intruding on something deeply treasured, yet Beatrice had invited her to examine one particular photograph. Her eyes darted from frame to frame until she found the one she sought.

A couple posed before a Christmas tree, smiling for the photographer. Eleanor picked up the frame and searched the branches. There! Five glass baubles decorated with mistletoe. Five! The entire set had once belonged to the Winterbournes. That could only mean that the friend Queen Victoria had gifted them to was none other than Beatrice's great-grandmother.

She did the maths quickly. Queen Victoria had died over 120 years ago. The dates fit the family timeline perfectly. How incredible—and yet Beatrice hadn't told her. Then again, she had said, 'Returned to me.' Maybe she hadn't just meant that her husband had repurchased the bauble, but that it had belonged to the family all along.

A wave of awe settled over Eleanor. What a piece of history to be proud of. No wonder Beatrice was in pieces now that it had been stolen.

Setting the photograph gently back onto the pianoforte, Eleanor glanced at a more recent picture of Mrs Winterbourne. "I'm going to help you get it back. I promise."

With a sigh, she turned to go back to bed—only to freeze in the doorway as she caught sight of a figure spinning away.

"Hey!" she called out without thinking.

She darted into the hall, eyes scanning left and right, but the corridor was empty.

"A ghost? Or am I just too tired?"

Heart aflutter, she hurried back to the safety of her room.

Chapter 10

NATHANIEL STEPPED INTO the drawing room, adjusting the cuffs of his shirt. The fire crackled in the hearth, casting long shadows over the antique furniture and heavy drapes. It was still early, and a grey December morning lingered beyond the tall windows, but Mrs Winterbourne was already waiting for him, seated in a high-backed chair as though presiding over a Regency-era parlour.

She looked him over as he entered, noting his modern clothes. "Mr Blackwood, you are out of costume."

Nathaniel smiled. "I thought it best to meet you as myself this morning. The game is over after all."

"Unfortunately, it is." She gestured for him to take the chair opposite. "You requested a meeting. Something tells me this is about more than the weekend's festivities."

Nathaniel hesitated only a fraction before nodding. "It is." He leaned forward in earnest. "Mrs Winterbourne, I need to be honest with you. When I first came here, I wasn't just here to play a part in the murder mystery."

"You thought perhaps this was some modern dating scheme?"

He laughed. "No, but what a marvellous idea. You could make a fortune setting up a singles version of the game."

Within her eyes danced a hundred questions, but she said nothing.

He pressed on. "I came here to write an article about you."

A flicker of something passed over her face—surprise, but not quite shock. She leaned back in her chair, "About me?"

Nathaniel nodded. "When I first heard about Winterbourne Hall, I was intrigued. But it wasn't just the house. It was you—the woman who purchased a grand but crumbling estate and transformed it into a Regency-style hotel. You live by a different set of rules. You don't just admire the past; you've chosen to live in it." He hesitated, then added, "And, if I'm being completely honest, I thought you might be a little eccentric."

Mrs Winterbourne let out a soft, knowing laugh. "Eccentric? That's a rather kind way of putting it, Mr Blackwood. I'm quite used to people thinking I'm mad. It doesn't trouble me anymore. Honestly, you should hear some of the things I've heard said about me when I walk into Willowcombe Village Store. 'The loony loon,' 'the woman who belongs in an attic,' 'the reincarnation of the first Mrs Winterbourne, sent to haunt them all'... The list goes on, and includes some descriptions I'd rather not repeat."

Nathaniel gave her a sheepish look. "So... I wasn't wrong?"

Her expression shifted, her self-deprecating replaced with something unreadable. "I note you talk in the past tense. Are you saying you're not writing this article now?"

Nathaniel shook his head. "Not without your permission."

For the first time since he started speaking, Mrs Winterbourne looked genuinely surprised.

"I should still like to write it," he continued, "but I'll only do so if you approve. I'll even let you read it before I submit it. If you don't like it, it won't be published."

She regarded him in silence for a long moment. "That is... unexpectedly considerate of you."

Nathaniel smiled. "You might even say uncharacteristic for a journalist."

Her lips twitched. "Quite." She tapped a gloved finger against the arm of her chair. "Very well, Mr Blackwood. You may write your article—but I will decide whether it sees the light of day."

"Agreed." He flipped open his notebook. "Shall we begin?"

Mrs Winterbourne sat a little straighter. "Ask your questions, then."

Nathaniel made a note. "Let's start with the house itself. Winterbourne Hall was in your family before you bought it back, wasn't it?"

A small smile played on her lips. "Yes, through my mother's line. It was built in the late 1700s and remained in our family for generations—until my grandfather lost it in the 1920s due to some unfortunate investments."

"But you brought it back?"

"I did," she said with quiet pride. "Two years ago, I had the opportunity to purchase it, and I did so without hesitation. Not everyone was pleased, of course."

Nathaniel paused. "Your son?"

Her lips pressed together briefly. "Philip believes I should have taken the money and invested it elsewhere. Something sensible, something secure. He thinks this house is a foolish venture."

"And instead, you turned it into a Regency hotel—and home?"

She gave him a knowing look. "You're wondering why I live this way."

Nathaniel chuckled. "I'd be lying if I said I wasn't curious."

Mrs Winterbourne let out a quiet breath. "When I was a child, I fell in love with Jane Austen's novels. The world she

151

described—orderly, elegant, full of wit and romance—it captured my imagination. It made life seem grander, fairer." She glanced away, her expression distant. "My own life... was not quite so charming."

Nathaniel didn't speak, sensing there was more.

"My husband, Jonathan Armitage, sent me away from our home," she said, her voice steady but laced with something bitter. "But he refused me a divorce. A scandal, you see. He could tolerate an absent wife but not a divorced one. I was left in limbo—neither married nor free. And with a son wholly under his father's thumb."

Nathaniel absorbed that quietly.

"When he died a little over two years ago, I sold his house in Chelsea and purchased Winterbourne Hall." She lifted her chin a touch. "Much to Philip's dismay. He saw it as throwing away his inheritance, and from the moment I put Jonathan's house up for sale, he has refused to speak to me."

Nathaniel tapped his pen against his notebook. "And would you do anything differently?"

Mrs Winterbourne considered the question, then gave a small, decisive shake of her head. "No."

"I thought not."

Uncomfortable talking about her son, she asked, "Are we finished?"

He hesitated. "One last question."

She raised an eyebrow.

"Who do you think stole your Christmas bauble?"

Her lips thinned, and for the first time, a flicker of genuine frustration crossed her face.

"If I knew that, Mr Blackwood, I would not be so troubled."

"Do you still suspect Eleanor?"

Mrs Winterbourne's expression softened. "Only a little."

Nathaniel relaxed. "I can assure you, she didn't steal it."

Her gaze locked onto his. "Oh?"

"I'd bet my life on it."

Mrs Winterbourne's lips twitched, just faintly. "I rather thought you might."

She sat back in her chair, thoughtful. "And yet, the bauble is still gone. More curious still—why take only that? There are far more valuable artefacts in this house. Whoever stole it… only wanted that particular item."

Nathaniel nodded. "A mystery indeed."

*****

Eleanor sat stiffly in the back of the car as it rumbled along the narrow country lane, the grey sky outside matched her mood. The prettiness of snow-kissed countryside did nothing to ease her stress. The butler, Mr Grady, drove in his usual unhurried manner, hands steady on the wheel, posture upright and proper as if even the simple act of driving must be performed with dignity.

They descended into Willowcombe Village, a postcard-perfect cluster of stone cottages, snow-topped hedges, and an old church with a square bell tower that dominated the skyline. The main street was quiet at this hour, save for the occasional villager going about their errands. Grady pulled up in front of a small, squat building of honey-coloured stone, its blue-painted wooden door bearing a modest brass sign: Willowcombe Village Police Station.

Eleanor sighed and climbed out.

153

"Would you like me to wait, miss?" Grady asked, ever the dutiful servant.

She shook her head. "No, thank you. I might be a while."

He gave a brief nod and pulled away, leaving her standing before the unwelcoming door.

Inside, the station was just as she imagined—cramped, dimly lit, and cluttered with filing cabinets whose drawers didn't quite close properly. A single desk sat to the left of the entrance, piled high with paperwork, behind which a middle-aged officer in a rather wrinkled uniform glanced up as she entered.

"Miss Carstone." He recognised her instantly, standing and motioning her to a door at the back. "If you'll come this way."

She was led into a plain interview room, its walls painted in an uninspiring shade of beige. A small table with two chairs sat in the centre, a tape recorder and notepad already placed on top. The officer gestured for her to sit, then took his own seat across from her.

"Right then," he said, flipping open the notepad. "Let's go through this again, shall we?"

Eleanor resisted the urge to groan.

Forty-five minutes later, she emerged from the police station feeling wrung out, as though she had been squeezed dry of any patience she had left. Though the questions had been much the same as before, there an undertone of quiet persistence in the officer's voice that set her on edge. They still suspected her.

As if to punctuate the thought, a headache began to take root behind her temples.

Pulling her coat tightly around her, she crossed the street to the village's general store, a narrow building with large display windows filled with tins of biscuits, boxes of tea, and neatly wrapped bars of soap. A small brass bell jingled as she pushed open the door, and a wave of warmth and the scent of baked bread washed over her.

Behind the counter, a buxom woman with greying curls and a floral-print blouse beamed at her.

"Oh, if it isn't Miss Carstone!" she cried, her voice full of good-natured nosiness. "Come for a bit of shopping, have we? Or are you escaping that grand old house for a breath of normality?"

Eleanor managed a weary smile. Having visited the store only once before, on the way to the Hall, she was amazed the woman remembered her. "Just some headache tablets, if you have them."

"Of course, dear, of course," the woman said, bustling over to a shelf and plucking down a small box. "And what a weekend you've had! The murder mystery! The theft! I bet you're all exhausted from it. I was saying to my sister just this morning, 'Now there's a group that won't be forgetting their visit in a hurry!'"

Keeping the box of tablets firmly in hand, Martha leaned on the counter, lowering her voice as though about to impart a great secret. "Course, my sister Maggie thinks I ought to keep my nose out of it. This morning, she said to me, 'Martha, you do have a long memory, but if you could keep your nosiness a little shorter, it would be good for all.'"

Eleanor bit back a smile. "And what did you say to that?"

"I said, 'You listen here, Maggie—having a long memory has got nothing to do with being nosey. That's just good sense. It's knowing what's what. Being nosey, on the other hand, is an art form, and some of us were just blessed with a gift.'"

Eleanor laughed. "And did Maggie agree?"

"Oh no," Martha said cheerfully. "She just muttered something about me knowing everyone's business before they do and went back to buttering her toast." She sighed dramatically. "She's never appreciated my talents."

Eleanor offered a polite nod, hoping the conversation had come to an end so she could prise that box of much-needed painkillers out of the shopkeeper's hand. Alas, Martha wasn't done.

"You know, I had a couple from the hotel in here last week—Mr and Mrs Dunlop, wasn't it? My word, they were the nosiest pair I've ever met! Asking all sorts of questions!"

Eleanor's head snapped up.

"Last week?" she repeated. "You mean they came in before the weekend?"

"That's right, lovely," the woman said, tilting her head in curiosity. "Why? You thought they popped in yesterday on their way home?" She let out a chuckle. "Oh no, dear. We're closed on Sundays."

Eleanor felt a prickle of unease.

Mr and Mrs Dunlop had claimed to know nothing about Willowcombe before arriving. But if they had been in the village last week, asking questions about the place...

Why had they lied?

*****

Eleanor arrived back at Winterbourne Hall just as Nathaniel was shrugging into his coat by the front door. He glanced up at the sound of her footsteps, giving her a quick, assessing look.

"Fancy stretching your legs?"

She hesitated, the worry of her second police interview still pressing on her shoulders. But fresh air sounded tempting—cleansing, and might help to alleviate her headache. "Give me a moment to put my boots on."

"Take your time," he said buttoning his coat. "I'll wait here."

Eleanor hurried upstairs to her room, quickly swapping her shoes for a sturdy pair of boots. As she pulled on her coat, she took a deep breath. The police still suspected her; she sensed it in the way they questioned her, and the way their eyes lingered on her a fraction too long. And yet, there was nothing she could do to prove her innocence—at least, not yet.

When she rejoined Nathaniel, he opened the door for her, and together they stepped out into the crisp winter air. They took the path that wound around the back of the house and led into the woodland beyond. Snow had settled in patches beneath the trees, and the bare branches above swayed in the wind.

After a few moments of companionable silence, Nathaniel glanced sideways at her. "How did your interview with the police go?"

Eleanor let out a dry laugh. "As well as can be expected."

"Did you ask them if they searched the secret passageway?"

She winced. "No."

Nathaniel stopped walking and turned to face her. "No?"

She sighed, tilting her face heavenwards as if hoping for divine intervention. "I didn't think it would help my case."

His brow furrowed. "Why on earth not?"

"Well," she shifted uncomfortably, "they already suspect me. If they knew that I knew a way to reach the bauble with the least chance of discovery, it would only add wood to their fire—which, frankly, I'd rather have put out."

Nathaniel was silent for a moment, then let out a low chuckle. "Eleanor, you do realise that sounds incredibly guilty, don't you?"

She groaned. "Yes, thank you, I'm aware."

He rubbed his gloved hands together, his breath misting in the cold air. "So what's your plan, then? Hope they stumble across it by accident?"

"No." She gave him a pointed look. "I was rather hoping you could pretend you only discovered it today and go to Mrs Winterbourne with the news. She could then call the police herself."

Nathaniel raised an eyebrow. "So you want me to take credit for your discovery?"

"I want you to be the innocent party presenting the information," she corrected. "I think you'll find the police are much more willing to believe an upper-class journalist who isn't already a suspect."

Nathaniel smirked. "I do enjoy how you turn my privilege into a useful tool."

She smiled sweetly. "It's about time it came in handy."

They continued their stroll, following the narrow woodland path. The Hall was now out of sight, the trees arching over them like a natural tunnel. The air smelled of damp earth and pine, and the sound of their footsteps was muffled by the soft ground.

"I actually have something to tell you," Eleanor said, glancing at Nathaniel.

"Oh?"

She hesitated, then decided there was no point in drawing it out. "When I stopped at the village shop, Martha—that is the owner, mentioned something interesting. Apparently, Mr and Mrs Dunlop came into the store last week."

Nathaniel slowed his pace mulling over the information. "Last week?"

She nodded. "And yet, they told everyone they had never been to Willowcombe before this weekend."

His expression darkened. "That's... not the kind of detail you get wrong by accident."

"Exactly."

Nathaniel let out a low whistle. "So either they lied, or Martha is mistaken."

"I'd bet on Martha. The woman might be nosey, but she doesn't seem the type to get her facts wrong—especially when it comes to people's comings and goings."

Nathaniel was quiet for a long moment. "This changes things."

"Yes is does. The question is... why were the Dunlops here before the weekend started? And what were they looking for?"

They walked on in thoughtful silence, the woods around them whispering in the breeze.

*****

The conservatory at Winterbourne Hall was a wintery sun-drenched sanctuary of glass and iron, its tall windows offering a panoramic view of the frost-kissed gardens beyond. Inside, the air was warm, scented with the earthy fragrance of potted citrus trees and the faint, lingering spices of the Christmas decorations that adorned the Hall.

Eleanor settled into a cushioned wicker chair, sighing as she curled her hands around a delicate china teacup. Opposite her, Nathaniel reached for a sandwich from the three-tiered stand, biting into it before giving an appreciative nod.

"Mrs Winterbourne took the news of the secret passageway rather well," he said between bites. "It came as quite the surprise, of course, but she was more delighted than anything."

Eleanor arched a brow. "Delighted?"

"Oh yes. She called it 'a most thrilling development' and began speculating on how many other hidden doors the house might have." He smirked. "I suspect I've only fuelled her romantic notions about her home."

Eleanor smiled. "And did she agree to ring the police?"

"Did it while I was still there. They're sending officers back to the Hall around four."

Eleanor stirred her tea, watching as the milk swirled into the rich amber liquid. "Good. At least that's one thing we don't have to handle ourselves."

Nathaniel chuckled. "For once."

They ate in comfortable silence for a moment, the clink of china and the occasional crackle of the fire in the adjoining drawing room the only sounds. The cream tea spread was impressive—an assortment of dainty sandwiches, scones piled high with clotted cream and jam, and an array of delicate pastries that looked almost too beautiful to eat. Almost.

As Eleanor reached for a scone, she leaned forward. "So, let's go over what we know about the Dunlops."

Nathaniel nodded, setting down his teacup. "Right. We now know they were in Willowcombe before the weekend officially began—something they conveniently failed to mention."

"Which suggests they were here for something other than the murder mystery."

Nathaniel reached for another sandwich. "Then there's Mr Dunlop's insistence on wearing gloves at all times."

Eleanor made a face. "Yes. I thought that was a bit over the top, even for a Regency weekend. Everyone else was willing to bend the rules now and then, but he never once removed them."

Nathaniel tapped his fingers on the table thoughtfully. "You know, that could mean something."

"Like what?"

"Maybe he had something on his hands he didn't want anyone to see," Nathaniel suggested. "A scar, an identifying mark... or even something as simple as ink stains. If he wrote something—say, a forgery—or handled something in a way that would give him away, keeping his hands covered would be a precaution."

Eleanor frowned, considering it. "It's possible, but you're speculating. It could mean that he didn't want to leave a single finger print behind. Let us keep to what we know. I still can't decide if he's behind this or if we're grasping at straws."

Nathaniel was quiet for a moment, then snapped his fingers. "Wait. I just remembered something."

Eleanor looked at him expectantly.

"Friday night, in the ballroom before dinner," he said, leaning forward, "the Dunlops were talking to that actor—what was his name? The one playing Lord Ambrose Whitmore."

"James Something," Eleanor supplied.

Nathaniel's eyes gleamed with interest. "Dunlop made a rather pointed comment about highwaymen—something about their way of stealing being *uncouth*."

Eleanor raised an eyebrow. "Well, he's not wrong."

"No, but think about it—what kind of person makes a comment like that? Not just someone who disapproves of crime, but someone with a particular attitude towards crime. He didn't say robbery was terrible or immoral. He said it was *uncouth*."

Nathaniel sat back, tapping a finger against his cup. "That's the kind of thing a high-class thief might say. Someone who considers himself above petty criminals. Someone who believes in a certain... finesse when it comes to stealing."

Eleanor's brow furrowed. "You think he was dropping hints about himself?"

Nathaniel shrugged. "Maybe. Or maybe he was just a little too confident—so assured that no one would suspect him, he got careless."

Eleanor considered this, biting her lip. "That would explain his general attitude. He always presented as more amused by the weekend than invested in it."

"Exactly. Like he was playing along, but not really playing."

They sat in silence for a moment, absorbing this new perspective. Outside, the winter afternoon was beginning to shift, the pale sky deepening as the sun made its slow descent.

"If he is behind the theft, how do we prove it and clear my name?"

"That is the question."

They both fell quiet, their thoughts tangling in the same frustrating loop. Somewhere in the distance, the grandfather clock in the hallway chimed three. One hour until the police returned. One hour to decide what to do next.

Chapter 11

THE CRUNCH OF TYRES on gravel signalled the arrival of the police, and moments later, six uniformed officers stepped out of their vehicles. Detective Sergeant Moffat led the group, his sharp eyes scanning the grand façade of Winterbourne Hall as though he expected to see the stolen bauble dangling mockingly from one of its many windows.

Mrs Winterbourne greeted them at the entrance, her expression as poised as ever, though Eleanor noticed the faint tightening around her mouth. Nathaniel stood beside Eleanor, his hands casually in his pockets, but she could tell from the way his jaw was set that he was bracing himself.

Once inside, Moffat wasted no time. "Mr Blackwood," he said, folding his arms, "I have to say, it's rather convenient that you only just discovered this secret passageway today. Almost as though you were covering for someone."

Nathaniel tensed. "I only discovered it today because I had no reason to look for it before. It's an old house. Hidden doorways and passageways aren't unheard of. With Mrs Winterbourne's permission I am researching the house."

Moffat raised a sceptical eyebrow. "And yet, Miss Carstone, who has been under suspicion, just so happens to know about it, too. You realise aiding and abetting is a crime, Mr Blackwood?"

Eleanor felt Nathaniel stiffen beside her. Not comfortable lying, she spoke up. "Detective, Nathaniel isn't covering for me. I didn't mention the passageway earlier because—" She hesitated, choosing her words carefully. "Because I am already under suspicion. I thought that if you knew I was aware of a secret way to access the room, it would only make me look guiltier."

Moffat studied her, then grunted. "Let's take a look, then."

The group made their way to the library. Nathaniel demonstrated how the passage was accessed, pulling at the hidden latch behind a book that released the panel. The officers filed in, torches in hand, illuminating the dust-laden walls of the narrow passage.

For the next half hour, they combed through the hidden corridors and the ballroom entrance, searching for any evidence the thief may have left behind. Eleanor held her breath as they dusted for prints, only to be met with disappointment.

"No usable fingerprints except for Miss Carstone's and Mr Blackwood's," one of the officers reported. "If anyone else used this passage, they were careful."

Nathaniel let out a frustrated sigh. "Which means the thief wore gloves."

Moffat grunted. "A professional job, then." He turned to Nathaniel. "You claim to be a journalist, Mr Blackwood. Surely you've put those skills to use. Any theories?"

Nathaniel exchanged a glance with Eleanor before nodding. "Actually, yes. We believe Mr and Mrs Dunlop may not be as innocent as they seem."

Moffat raised an eyebrow. "That sweet old couple? They are a bit doddering, don't you think, to pull off a heist of such quality."

"Appearances can be deceiving," Nathaniel said. "They were unusually interested in the value of Mrs Winterbourne's collection, Mr Dunlop never removed his gloves—not even to eat—and we've reason to believe they were in Willowcombe last week, meaning they may have scouted the Hall beforehand."

One of the younger officers let out a chuckle. "Sir, with all due respect, I don't think Mr Dunlop could tie his shoelaces properly, let alone pull off a heist."

Eleanor opened her mouth to protest, but Moffat held up a hand. "Enough." His expression was unreadable as he regarded both Eleanor and Nathaniel. Then, with an air of finality, he said, "I'm sorry, but I'm taking you both in for further questioning."

Eleanor's stomach clenched. "You can't be serious?"

"You were the one most interested in the bauble, paid even to pass on details of its authenticity!" Moffat stated. "And now we find only yours and Blackwood's fingerprints in the secret passageway. We need to be thorough."

He turned to one of his assistants. "I want a warrant signed off to search their rooms."

"You don't need a warrant," Nathaniel said evenly. "You have my permission to search my room. I have nothing to hide."

Eleanor nodded, her pulse thrumming. "And mine as well."

Moffat eyed them both before jerking his head at the staircase. "Fine. Let's get this over with."

*****

The Bluebell Parlour was a charming room but at that moment, it felt anything but inviting. Eleanor and Nathaniel sat stiffly on the settee while Detective Sergeant Moffat loomed nearby, his notepad in hand, waiting for his officers to complete their search upstairs.

Nathaniel let out a dry chuckle and leaned back against the cushions. "You know, Sergeant, when the bauble was stolen, you took everyone's fingerprints and searched all the rooms. Do

165

you think that if Eleanor or I had stolen it, we would now be tucking it away in the comfort of our beds?"

Moffat gave him a sharp look. "Criminals make mistakes."

"Yes," Eleanor said, "and so far, you have no evidence that we've made one."

Moffat didn't respond, but jotted something down in his notepad.

Eleanor turned to Nathaniel, lowering her voice slightly. "I still have a gut feeling about Mr Dunlop."

Moffat snorted but said nothing.

Eleanor turned back to the detective. "No, hear me out. I told you earlier that my client contacted me. He said that three of the baubles had already been stolen, and Mrs Winterbourne's might be next. That means whoever owns the fifth should be warned."

She hesitated, her thoughts suddenly aligning in a way that sent a thrill of realisation through her.

Nathaniel frowned. "What is it?"

Eleanor sat up straighter. "The only people who knew about this—at least, as far as I'm aware—were myself, you, and Mrs Winterbourne. But Mr Dunlop said something at lunch that didn't sit right with me at the time. He said, 'I am not certain why anyone would covet a collection of Christmas baubles.'"

Nathaniel stared at her. Then, his eyes widened. "How did he know the thief was stealing for a collection?"

Moffat's pen froze mid-scribble. A slow grin spread across his face, and for the first time since entering the room, he looked excited. "Are you telling me he said that in front of witnesses?"

"Everyone at the table heard it," Nathaniel confirmed.

166

Moffat snapped his notebook shut and strode to the door. "Stay here."

He marched out into the hall, his heavy footsteps echoing as he went in search of Mrs Winterbourne. Within moments, he returned, the lady of the house in tow.

"Mrs Winterbourne," Moffat said, "I need to confirm something with you. At dinner, did you hear Mr Dunlop say anything about the baubles being part of a collection?"

Mrs Winterbourne frowned, clearly replaying the evening in her mind. "Yes," she said after a pause. "I remember it quite clearly."

Moffat's eyes gleamed. "And did you, at any point, mention to any of your guests that the other baubles had already been stolen?"

Mrs Winterbourne glanced at Eleanor and Nathaniel before shaking her head. "No. The only people I discussed that with were Miss Carstone and Mr Blackwood."

Moffat's jaw tightened in satisfaction. "Then unless Mr Dunlop has some miraculous way of knowing things he shouldn't, he's just given himself away."

Eleanor leaned forward. "Is there any way to find out who owns the fifth bauble? They should be warned." Another thought came to her. "What if you lay a trap and catch Mr Dunlop in the act of stealing it?"

Moffat's grin turned wolfish. "Now that is an idea."

He turned on his heel, already issuing orders to one of his officers as he strode out of the parlour, leaving Eleanor and Nathaniel exchanging looks of triumph.

*****

167

The afternoon wore on, the winter light beginning to fade beyond the great windows of Winterbourne Hall. Eleanor and Nathaniel remained in the Bluebell Parlour, the fire crackling in the hearth as they waited for news.

To ease the tension of waiting, they played cards with Mrs Winterbourne while Debussy's soft, impressionistic melodies floated from the record player in the corner, soothing the stress of the afternoon.

It was nearing six when a car came up the long drive and stopped outside the grand, portico entranceway. Moments later, Detective Sergeant Moffat strode into the room, shaking the cold from his coat.

"Well," he said, his voice as dry as ever, "you were right about the Dunlops!"

Eleanor sat forward. "You searched their house?"

Moffat nodded. "Got a warrant and went through the place from top to bottom. We didn't find the baubles, but we did find enough evidence to make any barrister rub his hands together in glee. Maps, floor plans, notes on security weaknesses, sketches of alarm systems... It was all meticulously detailed. It is fair to say that Mr Dunlop takes his craft seriously."

Nathaniel let out a low whistle. "And Mrs Dunlop?"

Moffat gave a humourless chuckle. "Ah. Mrs Dunlop sang like a canary the moment we started questioning her. Claimed she had no idea what her husband was up to. Said she had simply thought he had a 'keen interest in architecture.'"

Eleanor's eyebrows shot up. "And the maps?"

"She insisted she thought they were for a book he was writing." Moffat shook his head. "Would have been a fascinating read—'The Gentleman Thief's Guide to England.'"

Nathaniel smirked. "And you didn't believe her?"

"Not for a second." Moffat leaned against the mantelpiece. "She knew. Maybe she didn't take part in the thefts, but she was fully aware of what he was doing. Which makes her an accessory."

Eleanor exchanged a glance with Nathaniel. "So, they're both in custody?"

"Indeed." Moffat folded his arms. "And between his meticulous notes and her desperate attempt to throw him under the carriage wheels, I'd say it won't be long before we track down the missing baubles as well."

Nathaniel sighed in relief. "So that's it, then? The case is closed?"

Moffat rubbed the bridge of his nose. "Dunlop's refusing to talk. So far, we haven't been able to locate the missing baubles."

Nathaniel frowned. "Not even at his house?"

Moffat shook his head. "No sign of them. But we did check the sat nav in their car, and it flagged something interesting." He pulled a notepad from his pocket, flipping through a few pages. "Yesterday, the Dunlops made a trip to Knutsford, Cheshire. We don't know who they visited yet, but it's the only location that stands out from their usual movements."

Eleanor's breath caught. "Knutsford?"

Nathaniel turned to her. "What is it?"

She hesitated, as if saying it aloud would make it all the more real. "It's just... my client lives in Knutsford."

A beat of silence passed as that information settled between them.

Moffat narrowed his eyes. "Your client?"

Eleanor nodded slowly, her mind racing. "The one who hired me to authenticate Mrs Winterbourne's bauble. Alistair Fenwick. He's a private collector. He's been acquiring items with royal provenance for years." Her voice dropped as the realisation struck. "And as soon as I confirmed Mrs Winterbourne's bauble was the genuine article, he knew it was worth stealing."

Nathaniel let out a low whistle. "So Dunlop wasn't working alone. Your client was his buyer."

Moffat's expression hardened. "It's starting to look that way." He closed his notepad with a decisive snap. "We'll need to pay him a visit. Obviously, without proof we only have a theory."

Eleanor folded her arms, a chill settling over her. She had taken pride in her work, in her ability to trace history through precious objects. But had she, unknowingly, played a part in this crime?

Nathaniel must have noticed her unease because he nudged her shoulder. "Hey. You didn't do anything wrong."

She nodded, though she wasn't sure she believed it.

Moffat turned to one of his officers. "Get a team ready. We're heading to Knutsford."

*****

After retiring for the night, Nathaniel sat at the antique writing desk in his room, fingers poised over the keyboard of his laptop, though his mind lingered elsewhere. The lamp beside him cast a warm glow, throwing long shadows over the dark wooden panels of the room. Beyond the heavy drapes, the night was still. Quietness had settled over Winterbourne Hall now that most of the guests had departed, but it was a deceptive quiet—beneath the surface, tension still simmered.

With a small shake of his head, he returned his attention to the screen. He had begun this part of the article intending to capture the grandeur of the estate, the traditions, the weekend's peculiar turn of events. But now, his words had taken on a different shape, a different focus.

There are those who might consider Mrs Winterbourne a relic of another time, a woman lost in history's embrace, much like the grand house she so carefully preserves. It is easy to see why—draped in her high-waisted gowns, speaking in the measured tones of an Austen heroine, she appears as one born not of this century but of another, plucked from the pages of a novel and placed, quite mistakenly, in modern-day Devon.

Nathaniel leaned back, considering the words. No, that was how he had once seen her, how many likely still did. But he had come to understand the truth.

Yet those who judge too quickly would fail to see the formidable mind behind the silks and muslins. Mrs Winterbourne is not a woman playing at history, but one who has made it her life's work to preserve it. She walks through the halls of Winterbourne not as a guest in the past, but as its guardian, breathing life into the stories etched within its walls. One need only look to her staff, all drawn into the Regency spell, each playing their part with a quiet reverence, as if time itself has folded in upon this house and granted them all passage to another age.

He hesitated before adding his next thought, fingers hovering before striking the keys.

She has known loss—such grief that might turn another woman cold, might harden the heart, make brittle what once was soft. And yet, it has done no such thing. Rather, she is kindness itself, a woman who, though she dwells among ghosts, extends warmth to the living. How admirable is she, this lady of Winterbourne, who asks nothing for herself and yet gives so freely to others.

Nathaniel ran a hand through his hair. He had not expected to write this, had not expected to feel this. Yet, the words rang true. With a final glance at the screen, he saved the document and closed the laptop.

*****

Eleanor sat cross-legged on the bed, her laptop open before her, but she hadn't typed a single word. The glow of the screen illuminated the deep furrow in her brow, the slight downward curve of her lips. A half-eaten biscuit rested on a saucer beside a cooling cup of tea—proof of her failed attempt to eat something, anything, to steady the roiling in her stomach.

She had come to Winterbourne Hall believing it would be an easy job. A straightforward authentication, a pleasant weekend in a grand old house, and then back to London with another successful assessment under her belt.

172

Instead, here she was, caught up in a heist, a suspect in a police investigation, and with a gnawing sense of failure clinging to her like a second skin.

But did this disappointment stem from this weekend's events? Or did her insecurities flow from everything that had come before?

She leaned back against the carved wooden back of the headrest, staring at the ceiling. It wasn't just the Mistletoe Bauble. It wasn't just the police or the lingering suspicion in their eyes. It was a lifetime of missteps.

She thought of her parents, and of the life that had been ripped away from her before she had even reached adulthood. A car accident. A phone call in the middle of the night. A hollow, crushing grief that had settled in her chest and never quite left. She had been packed off to London to live with her aunt—a kind woman, but one who had never wanted children and had never quite known what to do with her. Their relationship polite but distant. Her aunt had provided for her, but love? That had been harder to come by.

And so, in search of it, Eleanor had run headlong into her first romance—wild, desperate, foolish. She had let herself believe that love, real love, could be found in the arms of a man who whispered grand promises in the moonlight. She had followed him to Italy, imagining a life of passion and adventure, only to return six months later, heartbroken, humiliated, and thoroughly disillusioned.

Then there was the museum job—the one she had fumbled, the one she had walked away from with her confidence in tatters. She had meant well, but mistakes had piled up, and before she knew it, she was being kindly but firmly encouraged to seek opportunities elsewhere.

Authenticating antiques had been an accident. A fortunate one, perhaps the only fortunate one in her string of failures. Her old lecturer—patient, perceptive—had recognised something in her, had guided her on this path. And for once, something had gone right. She had found beauty in old things, in history, in the thrill of discovery.

And now even that was tainted.

Her chest ached with frustration. She had done nothing wrong, but the taint of suspicion clung to her. Worse than that, she had unwittingly led the thief straight to his prize. If she had never taken on this job, if she had never sent those photographs…

She shut her laptop with a sigh. There was no sense in going over it again and again. It wouldn't change the past.

But perhaps—just perhaps—there was still a way to make things right.

Chapter 12

ELEANOR SAT UP in bed with a start. The early morning light filtered through a gap in the curtains, casting a pale golden glow across the room, but she didn't notice it. An idea struck her, so simple yet so obvious that she could hardly believe she hadn't thought of it before.

Alistair Fenwick had lied.

He had told her his bauble had been stolen twenty years ago, but when she had searched through newspaper archives last night, she hadn't found a single mention of such a theft. That in itself wasn't conclusive—some thefts went unreported—but it seemed unlikely that a collector as wealthy and well-connected as Fenwick wouldn't have at least tried to recover something so rare.

Her old professor, Dr Harold Tinsley, had dedicated much of his career to tracking stolen antiquities. If anyone would remember a case like this, it was him.

Without wasting another second, Eleanor grabbed her phone from the bedside table and scrolled through her contacts. Dr Tinsley had always been kind to her, encouraging her when she had first stumbled into the world of antiques. He was one of the few people she still trusted implicitly.

She tapped out a message:

Good morning, Dr Tinsley,
I hope this email finds you well. I'm looking into a theft that supposedly took place around twenty years ago. A collector named Alistair Fenwick claims that a Christmas bauble, part of an original royal set, was stolen from him. I've searched

through the usual records but haven't found any
mention of the crime. Given your expertise, I
wondered if you might recall anything about it?
Best,
Eleanor

She hesitated only a moment before pressing send, then set her phone aside. Now, all she could do was wait.

A few minutes later, as she sat at the small desk in her room, her phone buzzed.

From: Dr Harold Tinsley
Dear Eleanor,
How wonderful to hear from you! I have to
confess, your email left me confused. If such a theft
had occurred, I would have expected some record
of it, particularly given the item's supposed royal
provenance. Are you certain of his claim?
Warm regards,
Harold

Eleanor's pulse quickened as she read the reply. That was it—proof that Fenwick had been lying.

But she needed to push him further. If he had gone to such lengths to collect the stolen baubles, he wouldn't want to be exposed as a fraud. If she offered to help him 'recover' his supposedly stolen bauble, he might just slip up.

She opened a new email.

From: Eleanor Carstone
Dear Mr Fenwick,
I've been thinking about our last conversation and wanted to offer my help. I understand how devastating it must have been to lose something so rare, especially when it holds such historical value. If you have any records of ownership—old photographs, insurance claims, or auction records—I may be able to assist you in tracking it down.
Let me know if you would be interested in my assistance.
Best,
Eleanor

She sent it before she could second-guess herself. Now, it was just a matter of seeing how he would respond.

Would he try to fabricate evidence? Brush her off? Or would his arrogance get the better of him and make him say something he shouldn't?

One way or another, they were about to get their answer.

*****

Eleanor entered the breakfast room to the comforting scent of bacon, eggs, and freshly brewed coffee. The rich aroma wrapped around her like a warm embrace, and for the first time in days, she felt properly hungry.

Nathaniel was already seated at a table near the window, a cup of coffee in hand, staring absently at the wintry landscape outside. At the sound of her approaching footsteps, he turned, his expression brightening.

"Good morning." He set his cup down. "You look... rested."

"I am." She slid into the chair opposite him. "And hungry."

"Now, that is a good sign. Shall we go all out and have the full English?"

She grinned. "Absolutely."

A short while later, steaming plates were set before them, heaped with eggs, bacon, sausages, black pudding, grilled tomatoes, mushrooms, and toast. Eleanor tucked in with enthusiasm, revelling in the simple pleasure of a proper meal.

Taking note of the rapidly disappearing food, Nathaniel grinned. "It's nice to see you enjoying your food again. I was starting to worry you were going to waste away before we solved this case."

She took a sip of coffee before replying, "Well, I think I might have done something useful this morning."

He raised an eyebrow. "Oh?"

She set down her cup. "I had an idea—one that might help draw out Fenwick. He told me his bauble was stolen twenty years ago, but I couldn't find any record of the theft. So, I emailed my old professor, Dr Tinsley, and he confirmed he has never heard of it either."

Nathaniel's brows lifted. "That's suspicious."

"That is what I thought. So I emailed Fenwick and offered to help him track it down. I asked if he had any proof of ownership—photographs, insurance records, anything that might help us 'recover' it."

Nathaniel's expression turned thoughtful. "Clever. If he tries to provide evidence, we'll know whether he's making it up. And if he refuses to engage, that's telling in itself."

"That's what I'm hoping."

Nathaniel lowered his fork. "So, do you think he ever owned it, or was that a lie to be able to employ you?"

Eleanor nodded as she finished a mouthful. "I think it is likely that he does own the bauble, which is why he wants all of them. But the theft never happened."

Nathaniel finished the last bite of his breakfast and sat back with a satisfied sigh. "Well, now that you've put your plan in motion, what do you say to taking your mind off it for a little while?"

"And how do you propose we do that?"

"A drive, fresh air, a change of scenery—maybe even a little walk if you're up for it."

She hesitated a moment before smiling. "That sounds perfect."

*****

An hour later, they were driving through the vast, windswept expanse of Dartmoor. The landscape was both bleak and beautiful, the rolling hills covered in frost and dotted with snow drifts, the sky a pale blue streaked with wisps of white cloud.

Eleanor rested her head against the window, watching the scenery blur past. She had forgotten how much she loved this place—how much it had once been home.

"You're quiet," Nathaniel remarked, his hands steady on the wheel.

She turned to him. "I was just thinking... my parents lived in Devon most of their lives. Me too, they died when I was fifteen. After that, I went to London to live with my aunt."

Nathaniel shot her a quick glance. "I didn't know that."

179

She shrugged. "It's not something I talk about often."

A moment of silence stretched between them, filled only by the gentle hum of the engine. "I'm sorry," Nathaniel said softly.

Eleanor shook her head. "You don't have to be. I wasn't looking for sympathy—I was just reminiscing. Being back in Devon this week has made me realise how much I love it here."

Nathaniel didn't press the matter, but she could tell he was considering her words. After a few more miles, he pulled the car into a layby near a footpath leading up onto the moor.

"Fancy a walk?"

Eleanor looked out at the rugged terrain, the low winter sun casting long shadows over the snow-covered bracken. The wind rattled the branches of a nearby tree, but the sight of the open landscape was too inviting to resist.

"Let's do it."

They stepped out into the crisp air, their breath misting in the cold. As they walked, Eleanor inhaled deeply, the freshness of low-growing shrubs, grasses and bog-mosses filling her lungs. It was freezing, but wild and invigorating.

Nathaniel glanced sideways at her. "So, do you think you might ever move back?"

She considered the question. "I don't know. Maybe." She kicked a pebble along the path. "I suppose I never let myself think about it before. London is... familiar. Safe, in a way."

"But does it still feel like home?"

She didn't answer immediately. Instead, she looked out over the rolling hills, the distant tors rising like ancient sentinels against the horizon.

"I don't think it ever felt like home."

Nathaniel smiled. "Well, that's something to think about, isn't it?"

She smiled back, and together, they continued walking across the moor, the wind whipping around them, carrying with it the promise of change.

As they reached the crest of a small hill, Eleanor pulled her phone from her coat pocket, her fingers tingling from the cold. She tapped the screen, but no notifications appeared. Frowning, she checked her signal.

"Nothing."

Nathaniel glanced at her. "No reply from Fenwick?"

"I don't know." She slipped the phone back into her coat pocket. "No signal out here." A sigh formed a white cloud in the air. "We should probably head back. If he has replied, I want to know what he's said."

Nathaniel nodded, turning them back toward the car. "Agreed. Let's see if the spider has wandered into the web you so cleverly set for him."

Eleanor smiled despite herself, falling into step beside him as they made their way down the path, the moor stretching endlessly behind them.

*****

By the time they arrived back at Winterbourne Hall, Eleanor's phone was back in range, and a notification popped up the moment they stepped inside. She stopped in the entrance hall, her stomach tightening as she saw the sender's name: Alistair Fenwick.

Without a word, she tapped the email open. Nathaniel, sensing the change in her, paused beside her.

181

Fenwick's message was short, but the tone was impossible to miss:

I THINK YOU HAVE ALREADY CAUSED ME ENOUGH TROUBLE. YOU WOULD DO WELL TO WATCH YOUR BACK. STAY OUT OF THINGS THAT DON'T CONCERN YOU.

All capitals, no polite sign-off. It looked rushed, almost frantic. And that last line—it sent a slow chill down Eleanor's spine.

Nathaniel read it over her shoulder. "Well, that's not suspicious at all."

Eleanor swallowed, steadying herself. "He's rattled. Do you think the police have interviewed him already?"

Nathaniel nodded. "It looks like it. And he's just given himself away. If he had nothing to hide, he would have brushed you off with some elaborate excuse, not…" He gestured at the screen. "*'Watch your back'?* That is not the response of an innocent man."

Eleanor's mind raced. "I need to forward this to Moffat."

Nathaniel squeezed her shoulder with a gentle touch. "Let's go find a quiet spot and do it now."

They walked through to the drawing room, where Eleanor sat at one of the writing desks and composed a quick email to Detective Sergeant Moffat, attaching Fenwick's reply.

Subject: Alistair Fenwick's Response
Detective Sergeant Moffat,
I emailed Fenwick this morning, offering to help him find his 'stolen' bauble and asking if he had

any proof of once owning it. His response was immediate and, as you'll see, not exactly subtle. It reads as though he was caught off guard, possibly even panicked.

I confirm that I have done some research and no report of his bauble has ever been made regarding its theft.

I'm forwarding his reply to you in case it's of use. Let me know if you need anything else.

Eleanor Carstone

She hit send and leaned back in her chair, exhaling. "Now we wait."

Nathaniel sat on the arm of the nearest chair, watching her. "You okay?"

"Yes," she said, though her pulse was still a little too fast. "I expected a response, but not one quite so... blatant."

Nathaniel folded his arms. "Blatant is good. Blatant gives Moffat something to work with."

Eleanor nodded, but unease still curled in her stomach. She had been expecting deception, misdirection—something clever. Instead, Fenwick had lashed out. That kind of reaction suggested he was no longer in control of the situation. And that made him dangerous.

*****

Eleanor's phone buzzed, the screen lighting up with Moffat's reply. She puffed out a breath, only just realising she had been holding it.

It wasn't much, but it was enough. She passed the phone to Nathaniel so he could read it, and he gave a small nod. "That's that, then."

Eleanor sank back into the sofa, releasing the last of the tension that had coiled in her shoulders for days. Nathaniel reached for the teapot and refilled her cup without asking, pushing it forward with a knowing glance.

"So." He stretched his arms behind his head. "How does it feel to no longer be a suspect in an international art theft?"

Eleanor let out a small laugh, shaking her head. "I'll let you know when I've had a full night's sleep."

He smirked. "How about we do something normal for a change? No mysteries, no police, no cryptic emails from criminal masterminds." He pointed at the fire. "We could just sit here and pretend we're guests at a country house party. Or we could drive into the village, grab a coffee, browse the bookshop. Your choice."

The idea of something normal, something completely removed from the chaos of the past few days, was surprisingly tempting. "The village sounds nice," she admitted. "But I think I just want to sit here for a bit. Warm fire, strong tea, no danger of being arrested. Plus it will be dark soon."

Nathaniel grinned. "A reasonable request." He lifted his teacup in a mock toast. "To uneventful afternoons."

They clinked their cups together.

A few minutes passed in companionable silence before the door opened, and Mrs Winterbourne stepped in. She was dressed, as always, in her impeccable Regency attire, though the delicate lace gloves suggested she had been working on something in her private study.

"I thought I might find you both here."

Eleanor straightened. "Do you have news?"

Mrs Winterbourne shook her head. "Not yet. But I wanted to thank you. Both of you." She crossed the room and settled into the armchair opposite them. "It's not every day a guest helps solve a real-life mystery. I must say, I didn't anticipate such stir when I planned the weekend."

Eleanor smiled. "Neither did we."

Mrs Winterbourne regarded her thoughtfully. "I know you'll both be leaving at the end of the week, but I want you to know that Winterbourne Hall will always have a place for you. Should you ever wish to return, in any capacity."

Eleanor's breath caught. It was a kind offer, but it also struck a deeper chord. Because despite everything—the theft, the police interrogations, the near-constant uncertainty—she had felt right here.

Nathaniel, sensing her hesitation, answered for both of them. "That's generous of you. We'll keep it in mind."

Mrs Winterbourne nodded, her usual serene smile in place, though something wistful lingered in her expression. "Good. That's all I wanted to say." She rose gracefully. "I'll leave you to your tea."

As the door closed behind her, Eleanor stared into the fire, the flickering light reflecting her own unsettled thoughts.

Nathaniel watched her. "Thinking about it?"

She glanced at him. "About what?"

"Staying."

She gave a small smile. "Not yet."

But she had a suspicion she had just lied, whether to him or herself she didn't know.

Chapter 13

THREE UNEVENTFUL DAYS LATER, the library was quiet but for the occasional crackle of the fire and the faint rustling of pages as Eleanor absently flipped through a book she wasn't reading. She had meant to puzzle through the missing *Northanger Abbey* again, but her mind was elsewhere: On the conversation with Beatrice, on the case, but mostly on the absent Nathaniel.

Once again, after breakfast with her, he had done a disappearing act leaving her on her own. Their short time together remained pleasant and companionable but she longer for something more. As the time of their departure drew closer, her hope of some sort of future with Nathaniel in it faded a little more.

The door creaked open, and Eleanor turned to see Mrs Winterbourne enter. She wasn't in her usual Regency gown but rather a soft blue dress, her hair pinned up in a way that made her look almost ageless. Draped over her arm was a coat.

Mrs Winterbourne smiled. "I was hoping I'd find you here."

"Is everything all right?"

"Yes, quite." She stepped further into the room. "I've just spoken with Detective Sergeant Moffat. The bauble has been recovered and is in police custody. It will be returned to me once everything is settled, but for now, it's safe."

"That's wonderful," Eleanor said, relieved. Without thinking she rushed forward and engulfed Beatrice in a hug. For a moment Beatrice was surprised but then she returned the hug squeezing Eleanor tightly.

When they pulled apart, Mrs Winterbourne glanced down at the coat she held. "I also wanted to give you something."

Eleanor frowned. "For me?"

Mrs Winterbourne lifted the coat. "This belonged to my grandmother. She lived in this house, you know, long before I was even a thought in my mother's mind. Of all the things my mother lost over the years, this was one of the few items she managed to keep hold of."

Eleanor's heart squeezed. "Beatrice, I can't possibly—"

Mrs Winterbourne held up a hand. "Now, now, don't say no just yet. I've been thinking of selling it, you see. A beautiful coat should be worn, not locked away in a trunk." She smiled with eyes full of empathy. "And I'd like to see it worn by someone who appreciates it. Sadly, it is too big for me."

The coat was a deep brown with gold embroidery that shimmered in the firelight. The intricate swirling patterns, shaped like vines and stars, had the delicate artistry of another era. The high collar and ornate brass buttons spoke of timeless elegance, and despite its age, the fabric looked as fine as the day it had been made.

Eleanor's breath caught. "It's beautiful."

Mrs Winterbourne smiled. "It's also warm. And I'd like you to have it."

For a moment, Eleanor hesitated, but the kindness in Beatrice's eyes left her with no choice. She reached out, running her fingers over the soft wool, and felt the history in it.

"Thank you," she said, her voice quieter than she intended.

Beatrice's smile warmed. "You are *very* welcome." After a pause, "So, you leave the day after tomorrow?"

Eleanor nodded.

"And do you mind if I ask…" She hesitated, though her eyes twinkled. "Are you and Nathaniel…?"

Eleanor let out a breathless laugh. "Oh, no, we're just—" She searched for the words. "Acquaintances. Thrown together by circumstance."

Beatrice laughed, shaking her head. "Oh, my darling child, you are certainly much more than that." She patted Eleanor's hand. "I do hope you both find your way."

Before Eleanor could think of a response, Beatrice turned, as if remembering something. "Now, since I've just given you a gift, I feel it only fair to ask for a favour in return."

"That depends on what it is."

Beatrice grinned. "Come and help me and Florence in the kitchen. We're making mince pies for tomorrow's party."

*****

Eleanor was still laughing when Mrs Florence Colepepper, the Hall's chubby and jolly cook, clucked at her, shaking her head. "Oh, you are a messy one, dear."

Eleanor wiped at the flour on her cheek, only for Beatrice to shake her head. "You missed a spot."

More laughter bubbled between them as the scent of cinnamon, nutmeg, and warm pastry filled the kitchen. The radio played Christmas carols, the faint crackle of an old recording giving the atmosphere a cosy charm. Outside, the frost clung to the windows, but in here, the heat of the ovens and the scent of rich spices wrapped around them like a festive embrace.

Florence, rolling out another batch of pastry, beamed at Mrs Winterbourne. "You know, we could do more of these Christmas Balls next year. The guests seem to like them best."

Beatrice nodded thoughtfully, cutting out circles of dough. "Yes, I was thinking the same. The events are funding the restoration, but slowly."

"Then more Christmas Balls it is," Florence declared.

Eleanor dusted her hands off, watching them with quiet admiration. This place—this home—was a piece of history, but it was also alive. Beatrice had breathed life into it. The thought of more Christmases here, of the Hall filled with music and laughter, warmed her in a way she hadn't expected.

She reached for a marshmallow to drop into her hot chocolate, catching Beatrice's eye as she did.

For the first time in a long while, she felt something close to belonging.

These people had become more than just acquaintances.

And Nathaniel Blackwood?

In time, she hoped she would forget him because unrequited love hurt.

*****

Thirty-five miles from Willowcombe, Nathaniel hesitated outside his sister's cottage, his breath misting in the cold air. He wasn't sure why he had come—not exactly—but the moment he left Winterbourne Hall that morning, his car found its way here of its own accord. He needed answers. Or at least, someone to make sense of the questions he didn't know how to ask.

Anna opened the door with surprise, taking one look at his face before stepping aside. "Come in before you freeze."

He stepped into the warmth of the little cottage, shaking off the cold and unbuttoning his coat. The delicious aroma of baking cookies filled the air, while a fire crackled in the log-burner bathing the room in a golden glow.

She folded her arms. "Well, I knew this day would come."

Nathaniel frowned as he shrugged off his coat. "What day?"

"The day you turned up on my doorstep looking like a man in turmoil." She smirked. "And judging by that look, it's a woman."

He let out a dry laugh. "That obvious, is it?"

She led him to the sitting room, waving him into the armchair. "I'm your sister. I know things." She gave him a pointed look as she went to put the kettle on to make a pot of tea. "So, who is she?"

Nathaniel ran a trembling hand through his hair. "Her name's Eleanor."

Anna popped tea bags into a teapot and leaned back against the counter. "Tell me about her."

He hesitated, but then the words came, unbidden. "She's clever—witty, even when she's exasperated. She has a way of seeing people, of understanding them. And she's braver than she gives herself credit for." He stared at the logs behind the glass front of the burner. "But I barely know her."

Anna studied him over the rim of her cup. "And yet here you are, tormented over her."

"That's what I don't understand." He leaned forward, his elbows on his knees. "It's been days, Anna. Days! I haven't had time to get to know her, but it feels…" He let out a sharp breath, shaking his head. "It feels like I do. In the last few days I could have spent time to get to know her better. Instead… I found myself running away, hiding in work and long walks."

"Yet still not able to get your thoughts clear." Anna was quiet for a long moment before she added, "Sometimes, knowing someone isn't about time. It's about recognition."

Nathaniel frowned. "What do you mean?"

She smiled faintly. "There are people we meet who feel like strangers, even after years. And then there are those we meet who feel familiar, as though we've known them far longer than we have."

He didn't answer. He wasn't sure he could.

Anna took the boiling kettle and poured water into the pot. Then picking up a tray she came in and sat down opposite him on the living room sofa. "What's stopping you?"

Nathaniel stiffened. He hadn't meant to say it out loud, but the words were there, hanging between them. "Claire."

His sister's expression softened as she poured them both a cup of tea.

"I married young. Too young, probably. But I loved her, Anna. And then—" He broke off, his throat tight. "Five years. That's all we had."

"I know."

"When she died, I thought—" He let out a slow breath. "I thought I'd never survive it. That I'd never let myself be that vulnerable again." He looked up at her. "What if I'm right? What if it happens again?"

Anna held his gaze. "What if it doesn't?"

He swallowed hard.

She leaned forward, resting a hand on his arm. "You're allowed to love again, Nathaniel. It doesn't mean you love Claire any less. It just means you're still here."

Nathaniel sat back, staring at the fire, his mind a tangle of thoughts. He wasn't sure what he would do.

But he knew he had a choice to make.

Chapter 14

MISS ELEANOR CARSTONE had not intended to become a thief.

Yet here she stood in the walled rose garden of Winterbourne Hall, snowflakes catching in her dark curls and the winter air crisp against her cheeks—having narrowly escaped being charged with the theft of a most treasured item.

Wrapped in the luxurious brown coat Mrs Winterbourne had gifted her, she walked through the gardens making her goodbyes to the bleak landscape she had come to love. The cream scarf at her throat, soft as a whisper, fluttered in the breeze with each step.

Fate, it seemed, had *not* brought her to Winterbourne Hall to steal the Mistletoe Bauble—but to help find it!

A small breath escaped her, clouding before her. Beneath her boots, the path had been swept clear of snow, but the rose bushes lining either side stood skeletal and bare, their twisted branches holding only the memory of past summers. She could almost imagine it as it once had been—vibrant, lush, and heady with the scent of a hundred blooming roses. In the golden light of late afternoon, ladies in Regency gowns might have wandered here, parasols open against the sun, whispering secrets to their suitors.

But today, it was silent, save for the soft hush of snowfall and the distant call of a robin redbreast that pecked at the soil ahead of her.

In coming here, Eleanor found that not only had she helped discover the bauble, but she had found the courage to change her life. No longer would she hide from meeting new people, she determined that from this week forward she would enjoy life more. For although Nathaniel made it clear by his absence he didn't want a romantic relationship with her, he had helped her come out of her shell.

They had solved the murder mystery game together. They had uncovered the truth of the real heist. But ever since their argument, something between them had remained unsettled. The ease, the warmth, the unspoken promises—they had been replaced with careful words and lingering silences.

She tilted her face to the sky, eyes closing briefly as the cold kissed her lashes. Perhaps it was for the best.

A fresh gust of wind sent a flurry of snow across the garden, and she turned to go back to the house, striding now, intent on returning to the Hall before the snowfall thickened.

*****

Nathaniel arrived back at Winterbourne Hall to find it emptier than he had expected. The reception desk was empty, the corridors quiet. The fire in the drawing room crackled warmly, but something was missing.

Eleanor.

He hadn't seen her since the morning, and the knowledge sat uneasily with him. After everything they had been through, he couldn't let things end like this.

A question to Mr Grady sent him marching to the gardens. It had started snowing in earnest now, fat, lazy flakes drifting down from the grey sky. He tucked his hands into his coat pockets, moving past the frozen fountain and along the path in a hurry to reach the walled rose garden.

And then—there.

A lone figure, wrapped in a deep brown coat, walked steadily through the snowfall.

He exhaled, something in his chest easing.

"Eleanor!"

She glanced up at the sound of his voice, surprise flickering across her face before she masked it. "Nathaniel."

He caught up to her, shaking the snow from his hair. "What are you doing out here?"

"Taking a walk. What are you doing out here?"

"Looking for you."

Her lips parted, but she said nothing. The wind stirred the ends of her scarf, and she lifted a gloved hand to tuck it closer against her throat.

Nathaniel hesitated. The magnitude of all they hadn't said passing between them. Then, as another gust of wind sent snow dancing between them, he reached for her hand.

"Come on," he said, nodding at the gazebo. "Let's take shelter."

She could have refused him. She should have, perhaps. But something in his eyes held her still, and before she quite realised it, she was following him.

The gazebo, though open on all sides, still offered slight shelter from the falling snow. Ivy twisted around its wooden posts and beams, and the scent of damp earth and old roses lingered beneath the crisp winter air.

Eleanor leaned back against one of the posts, her hands buried in her coat pockets. Nathaniel stood before her, his expression unreadable.

At last, he let out a slow, unsteady breath. "I don't want to leave things like this."

She let out a small, bitter laugh. "Like what?"

"Like we're strangers again."

She looked away. "Maybe that's what we are."

"No," he said firmly. "We're not."

Snow gathered in the folds of her scarf, dusted the dark strands of her hair. She felt it melting against her skin, cool and fleeting, and still, she refused to meet his gaze.

Nathaniel stepped closer. "Eleanor, I—" He hesitated, ran a hand through his hair, sighed. "I was an idiot. I never should have doubted you, not for a moment."

She swallowed, throat tight. "No, you shouldn't have."

He gave a small, wry smile. "I see we're in agreement."

Silence stretched between them. A breeze sent a fresh flurry of snow into the gazebo, and Eleanor shivered. Nathaniel reached into his coat pocket and pulled out a small sprig of mistletoe, snipped from the fireplace wreath. With careful fingers, he fastened it to a wooden beam above them.

"I know it's not quite Queen Victoria's Christmas Bauble. But it is mistletoe."

She glanced up, her lips parting in surprise, then back at him. His expression tender, laced with something deeper, something unspoken.

Nathaniel reached over and brushed snowflakes from her hair.

Her breath hitched.

His hand lingered, fingertips tracing the damp strands at her temple before sliding to cup the side of her face.

"I don't want this to be the end," he murmured.

She searched his eyes, the blue deeper than the winter sky, and realised—despite everything, despite their arguments, their missteps, her stubborn pride—she didn't want it to be the end either.

Her gloved hand lifted, resting lightly against his chest.

Nathaniel inhaled sharply, as though the contact had undone something inside him. And then—

He kissed her.

It was the kind of kiss written in stories, the kind that stole breath and time, that banished the cold and turned winter into warmth. His arm slid around her waist, drawing her closer, while his other hand cradled the back of her neck, his thumb tracing the delicate line of her jaw.

Eleanor melted against him, into him, her fingers curling into the fabric of his coat. Snowflakes tangled in their hair, settled on their shoulders, disappeared against the heat between them.

When they broke apart, his forehead rested against hers, his voice barely above a whisper. "Well," his lips curved into a smile. "Eleanor Carstone, I do believe you've pulled off the greatest heist of all."

"Oh?"

"My heart."

Eleanor laughed softly, her hands tightening against his coat. "You should have kept it under lock and key."

He grinned. "Too late for that."

The second kiss was fuelled by their passions as they pressed against one another hungry for love.

By the time they parted for the second time, her lips were flushed, her breath uneven, her heart pounding wildly against her ribs.

"So," he said, voice low, teasing. "Are we still pretending we're strangers?"

Eleanor laughed, "Shut up, Nathaniel."

He grinned. "Make me."

So she did.

Epilogue

Twelve Months Later

The cottage glowed with warmth, its low-beamed ceiling draped with evergreen garlands, the scent of mulled wine and spiced oranges filling the air. A fire crackled in the hearth, casting golden light over the snug living room, where the last remnants of their preparations for the evening lay scattered around.

Eleanor stood before the mirror, adjusting the drape of her ivory shawl over the delicate lace sleeves of her Regency gown. It had been twelve months since she had first stepped into Winterbourne Hall, twelve months since the heist, the game, and the moment that had changed everything. A year ago, she had stood in that grand ballroom believing fate had led her there to steal a bauble. Instead, it had brought her to Nathaniel.

She turned at the sound of his voice.

"Do I look the part?" Nathaniel emerged from their bedroom, dressed in full Regency attire—tailcoat, cravat, and a waistcoat in deep blue that only made the warmth in his eyes more striking.

Eleanor smiled. "Ridiculously so."

He struck a mock-heroic pose, one hand at his waist. "It is, after all, a Regency dinner. One must commit fully."

She shook her head with fond amusement and reached for the clasp of her necklace, fumbling with it. Without a word, Nathaniel stepped behind her and fastened it, his fingers warm against her skin. As he did, her gaze caught on the glint of her ring in the firelight—an antique diamond set in a delicate band, as timeless as the love it represented.

Catching her gaze in the mirror, Nathaniel grinned. "Admiring your spoils, Miss Carstone?"

"Hardly stolen!" She laughed and turned to face him. "Acquired under perfectly respectable circumstances."

He took her hand, pressing a kiss to her fingers. "I still can't believe you agreed to marry me."

She tipped her head to the side. "It took you long enough to ask."

He laughed and pulled her closer. "We're late, we should leave soon, or Mrs Winterbourne will assume we've been caught up in some great scandal."

"She wouldn't be wrong," Eleanor teased, but she reached for her cloak, nonetheless.

Nathaniel took it from her, shaking it out before wrapping it around her shoulders. "You're sure she won't mind if you're late? Seeing as you work for her now?"

Eleanor adjusted the folds of the heavy fabric, smiling. "She'll forgive me. I found her the most exquisite Georgian tea set this week—she's rather pleased with me."

Mrs Winterbourne tempted Eleanor away from London, giving her a reason to stay in Devon when she offered her a position to help restore the Hall to its former glory eleven months ago.

Eleanor sourced antiques, uncovering treasures hidden in dusty auction houses, and ensuring every piece that returned to Winterbourne had a story worth telling. She had never imagined such a life before, yet now she couldn't picture anything else.

With Eleanor intent on leaving London, Nathaniel decided to use his savings and take a year off work to write a novel.

The pair of them connected by a sixth sense gazed at the letter on the mantelpiece—his agent's letter. The publishing house wanted his book.

He laughed. "A year ago, I was writing exposés. Now, I'm writing novels. I blame you entirely."

Eleanor feigned innocence. "I've done nothing."

Nathaniel leaned in, his breath warm against her cheek. "You made me believe it was possible."

She smiled, her heart full, and together they stepped out into the night, hand in hand, ready to return to Winterbourne Hall— not as strangers drawn by secrets, but as a couple with a future ahead of them.

*****

Winterbourne Hall shimmered like a dream against the frost-laced night, its windows aglow with golden candlelight. From inside, the sound of laughter, the lilting strains of a string quartet, and the occasional chime of crystal against crystal floated into the crisp December air.

Eleanor stepped from the carriage, the cold nipping at her cheeks. She adjusted her cloak, shaking off a dusting of snow, and turned to Nathaniel, who offered his hand with a smirk.

"Well, Mrs Blackstone," he said as she took it, "shall we return to where it all began?"

She rolled her eyes, though a smile curved her lips. "Try not to get us tangled in another mystery this time, won't you?"

"I make no promises."

The grand entrance was alive with familiar faces—Mrs Winterbourne, gracious as ever in deep emerald silk, Mr Grady directing guests with a flick of his gloved hand, and a few returning guests from last year's infamous gathering. But there were new faces as well, including one that Eleanor had been particularly looking forward to seeing.

"Nathaniel," she said, turning. "There's someone I want you to meet."

Across the entrance hall stood a fragile-looking woman in a flowing gown of soft grey, her dark curls pinned elegantly beneath a cluster of holly and pearl-headed pins. She was speaking to Mrs Winterbourne but turned as Eleanor approached.

"Isabel!" Eleanor greeted her warmly, touching her arm. "I'm so pleased you decided to join in after all."

"You persuaded me. Now that I see everyone in their full regalia I understand what you mean. I shall be painting this scene at first light."

Eleanor turned to Nathaniel. "Nathaniel, meet Isabel Farnham. She's a wonderful artist—her floral studies are breath-taking."

Nathaniel gave a courteous nod. "A pleasure, Miss Farnham. Are you working on a new collection?"

"She is," Eleanor answered for her, excitement in her voice. "And where better than Winterbourne Hall to paint winter blooms?"

Isabel smiled. "And where better than a grand Regency ball for inspiration?"

Before Nathaniel could respond, the warm hum of conversation was shattered by a piercing scream.

The entire room seemed to freeze.

A woman, pale and shaking, stood at the entrance to the Bluebell Parlour, one gloved hand pressed to her mouth. "My brother—" she gasped. "He's dead!"

203

The string quartet faltered into silence. Murmurs spread like ripples in a pond.

Eleanor's breath caught.

Nathaniel turned to her. "I didn't know there was a game on this evening."

She shook her head. "There isn't."

"Well, that didn't take long for the next puzzle to emerge."

She shot him a look, but the corners of his lips twitched in the way they always did when trouble loomed on the horizon.

Mrs Winterbourne was already striding forward, calm and composed. "Mr Grady," she said firmly. "See that the doors are locked at once."

A chill ran down Eleanor's spine, though whether from the cold draught caused by the swinging door or the unmistakable rush of another mystery, she couldn't say.

The End

Thank you so much for reading *The Mistletoe Heist*. I hope you enjoyed Eleanor & Nathaniel's Christmas mystery.

If you have time to leave a review, I would really appreciate it; reader's words of encouragement mean the world to me.

Sincerely, Tracy

P.S. Isabel Farnham's story can be found in *The Hollywreath Murder*

Stay Updated

The Mistletoe Heist is the first book in the Winterbourne Cosy Mystery series.

You might find Tracy's website handy if you would like to know what she's up to next: https://tracytraynor.wordpress.com

☺

You can find all of Tracy's books here:
https://www.amazon.com/stores/Ms-T-N-Traynor/author/B01EIJB70K

☺

If you would like updates on Tracy's latest releases, you can receive her no spam newsletters at: https://sendfox.com/tntraynor

☺

As well as the latest deals, BookBub has a new release alert. If you'd like to, you can follow Tracy here:
https://www.bookbub.com/profile/t-n-traynor

☺

Facebook:
https://www.facebook.com/profile.php?id=100064909182534

Printed in Great Britain
by Amazon